SMALL
STATIONS
FICTION

Abel TOMÉ

NIGHT OF THE WOLF

Published in 2023 by
SMALL STATIONS PRESS
20 Dimitar Manov Street, 1408 Sofia, Bulgaria
You can order books and contact the publisher at
www.smallstations.com

This book was first published in the Galician language as *A noite do lobo* by Editorial Galaxia (Vigo, 2019). Chapter titles are taken from Emily Dickinson's poetry. A list of our fiction titles can be found at www.smallstations.com/fiction

The cover image of a wolf is from the thirteenth-century manuscript *De Natura animalium* (Ms. 711) kept in the Bibliothèque municipal de Douai, but formerly part of the Marchiennes Abbey collection, folio 13r. The image has been provided by the Bibliothèque virtuelle des manuscrits médiévaux (IRHT-CNRS) and is used with permission

 XUNTA
DE GALICIA

*This work received a grant from the Ministry of Culture, Education and University of the Xunta de Galicia*
*Esta obra recibiu unha subvención da Consellería de Cultura, Educación e Universidade da Xunta de Galicia*

ISBN 978-954-384-141-7

Abel TOMÉ

*Night of the Wolf*

WINNER OF THE ILLA NOVA AWARD FOR FICTION

English translation by Jonathan DUNNE

Small Stations Press

*For her,*
*subjected,*
*who never knew love,*
*who was never kissed.*

*'Tis not that Dying hurts us so –*
*'Tis Living – hurts us more.*
Emily Dickinson

## 'TIS NOT THAT DYING HURTS US SO

First, it was the spark. The flame rising in vibrant colours. Then, the blaze. Fire.

The mist of Luiçiana oppresses the landscape. It's thick. White. Turns the world into a void. As it was in the beginning. A little piece of paper without ink. Nothing. Nothing at all. I suppose.

Nobody sets foot outside. When there is mist, you don't leave the house. It's an invisible rule everybody has etched on their brains. Mothers warn their children about it when they're small. They huddle around the fire while warming their bodies with cabbage and potato soup. That's the aim. To warm the insides with something. Grandmas recall worse times. I doubt there were worse times than this. Every day, a fight begins, and another ends. That's war for you. *Kings* wishing to subject other *Kings*. Tenants who rebel. The Church forcing savages to believe. In the end, there are just nameless corpses piled up at the edge of some hill. Bloody bodies carried by the current of a river on the other side of the world. A family weeping for the death of a child they were unable to bury properly. And in capital cities, in front of a good breakfast, under the ceiling of an exquisitely furnished room, Ministers signing peace treaties while planning another act of butchery. We're just chess pieces to them. Wooden figures that fall on the board. Once the game is over, back to the beginning.

This winter is too cold and damp. It reminds me of days in the *jungle*. It wasn't cold there, but the humidity was overwhelming. I found it difficult to swallow air the first few weeks. It was like breathing a nightmare. After a while, the body gets used to the change. Now even the dampness of Luiçiana seems light to me. The wood is thick and old. Like it was in the *jungle*. We had to clear a path through hostile, unfamiliar vegetation. Days later, coming back the same way, the path had disappeared. It was all covered over again. Back to the beginning. Lots of people say the worst thing about the *jungle* is ignorance. Not knowing who you're going to meet. Hundreds of tribes with hundreds of bloody rituals. It's not true. The worst thing about the *jungle* is the *jungle* itself. The rebellious forest that seems to trap your feet. As if every element was aware of an enemy approaching. We were the enemy.

Luiçiana is solitary, but pleasant. The neighbours do their own thing and don't ask many questions. Silent people. But despite the little they have, they are kind and generous. Every family possesses a piece of land. In most cases, it doesn't provide much. The families are large. Grandfathers, grandmothers, fathers, mothers, and too many children... Lots head off to the cities. They're tired of working an acidic, infertile land. All the same, I can rest here. I don't need much to reach the end of the day. This year, the harvest was good. Besides, one thing Luiçiana does have is roe deer and boar. People here find it difficult to catch them. For me, it's simple. Hunting an animal is like hunting a man. That's something you don't forget. What are we, if not animals?

Tac-tac tac, tac-tac tac, tac... A horse stopped in front of the door. Somebody got off and landed in the mud. Took one step and then another. Looked at the door and banged on it. I went tense. I rushed to grab my knife and hide it up my sleeve.

"Who is it?" I shouted.

"I have a message for Lourenço d'Ourantes. Are you Captain Lourenço d'Ourantes?"

I hadn't heard that bit about "captain" for some time. A shiver ran down my spine. Made my body tremble. I heard the shouts in my head again. Sticking into the depths of whatever we have inside like needles. The shouts. Once again. They will pursue me until my death.

"There's nobody here with that name. Go away!"

"Captain d'Ourantes, I have a message for you. It's urgent. I beg you to open, sir. It's very cold out here. I've been travelling for nine days. I've barely eaten. I entreat you to give me a bowl of soup next to the fire."

"Go to the town. You'll find food and a warm bed there. Leave me alone."

"I have to deliver the message, milord. It's my obligation. Do this for a comrade in Her Majesty's troops."

There is a code among combatants on the same side. If one of them asks for help, you have to give it. I didn't know whether that stranger soaked in cold and fear was lying. Behind the door, I wasn't going to find out. I'm not a coward. It's not that. But you never know. There are lots of people who seek my death. It's true that I deserve to die, but not at the hands of just anybody.

I approached the entrance, gripping the knife hidden up my sleeve. I opened the half-rotten wooden door. On the other side was a boy in his *twenties* dressed in fine clothes. Too young to be a fighter. He was trembling with cold. I imagine it was because of the cold. He had a sword hanging off his hip and a hat adorned with the long feather of an exotic bird. Such clothes were not fashionable at that time. Nor was carrying a sword. It's also true that the southern counties are worlds that follow another style. Do their own thing. Are slightly backward. The way of treating people is different. They say words like "milord" and "master", as if they were someone's property. A dog. They maintain an ancient, excessively lordly language. From the past.

"I beg to be allowed in. I need to warm myself by the fire. I think I'm more in the other world than this one."

"You're not wearing the right clothes to be travelling to Luiçiana on horseback. You should have thought about that before you left wherever it was you came from. Come in."

The lad entered quickly and rushed towards the fire. During winters in Luiçiana, the fire doesn't go out. It's always there, suspended, gorging on the firewood that is collected in summer. Eternal. It can stay lit for months until well into spring. Large families don't get warm with the heat emanating from their bodies. Although the dwellings are small, it's important to have a fire going for as long as necessary.

"Here. It's deer stew. It's somewhat bitter. I'm not a great cook. Even so, better this than nothing."

The boy grabbed the plate and the spoon and started eating compulsively. I watched him from above, while he continued gorging the stew on his knees. He hadn't even taken off his hat and gloves. He was wearing black leather boots. They were caked in mud.

"Many thanks, Captain d'Ourantes. I hadn't eaten in days."

"Don't call me that."

"Wh... what?"

"Don't call me that. Captain. Don't use that term. I'm not a captain. I haven't been one for a while."

I offered the boy a seat. My house is poor. Like almost all the houses in these parts. I have the bare minimum. I placed a stool next to him and sat on another I had made a few months earlier from a piece of oak. I tried to carve it extremely carefully, but the truth is I don't have the patience. Never have done. That's why my father packed me off to the army. To bear arms. He knew I would make a terrible blacksmith, herdsman, shoemaker, peasant... He knew I was fit for war. A body that serves only to kill or to die on the battlefield. To bleed or be bled dry. He was not mistaken.

"All right then. What's your name?"

The boy looked at me with a cat's eyes. I don't know whether they were happy because his belly was full, or fearful. He put down the plate. Took off the hat and placed it next to the fire. He did the same with the gloves.

"My name is Johan Pelaiz, sir. I have a message for you from the Count of Constança. Misfortune has tainted our land. We need your help. My lord will pay you handsomely."

"The Count of Constança?"

"Yes, sir. Ricardo de Guimaraes, Count of Constança Valley. In the south. It's a small county full of streams. Extensive woods. And wild animals. My lord's family is highly regarded by the *Queen*. They have served the crown and *God* loyally for centuries."

I knew Constança Valley because of the war. Afonço Gonçalves and Tirso de Ledo fought at my side in the *jungle*. They both died there from arrows poisoned by savages. And they were both from the aforementioned county. They didn't speak well of their lord at the time. They said he killed people with hunger. The taxes were very high, and the peasants worked the Count's lands day and night. That was a long time ago. In Luiçiana, there hasn't been a landowner for some time. The law of the people took over here. There was a rebellion, and they cut off his head. The rest of his body was hung by the legs at the entrance to the old castle. It stayed there until the vultures had stripped it of meat. They also kicked out the clergy. Emptied the monastery pantries and shared the foodstuffs among the villagers. Sometimes the people of Luiçiana remind me of savages. Despite their serenity, they have a devastating blaze inside them. They fight tooth and nail. They don't care about the consequences. That's why I came here. One way or another, Luiçiana is the *jungle* on this side of the world.

"What does your lord want from me?"

"My lord Count desires your services. Your skills have been well known ever since you came back from the *Queen's* troops."

"What skills?"

The boy lowered his head and then looked at me as if he didn't understand a thing. He turned his body and rolled up his sleeves. He placed his palms in front of the fire and then turned back. Let out a sigh of satisfaction.

"Si… sir. You are Lourenço d'Ourantes, the wolf hunter. In our land, your skills as a hunter are better known than as a captain, if you'll permit me to say this, sir."

"It seems you know a lot about me, boy. Less than you think. I haven't been involved with that kind of thing for quite some time. Wolf hunter. That was a long time ago. Now I just want to rest until my hour comes."

The boy's words reminded me of the last time. The last act of butchery. The last wolf. The disaster in White Cliffs. White Cliffs is the *jungle*. The *jungle* is White Cliffs. Two places that wear away at me and turn me into sand. Man's metamorphosis into soil. What we once were. I won't forget it even after I'm dead. That must be hell. *Self-destruction* brought about by memory. Again and again, again and again, again and again… and so on until eternity.

"I know, sir. We all know what happened in White Cliffs. It's a familiar story."

I suddenly stood up. Glared at the boy with blazing eyes. With an enraged gesture. As if I was a bolt of lightning. It's enough the way I torture myself, I don't need a stranger to remind me of my obsessions and throw them in my face.

"Tell your lord Count I don't want anything to do with him. You can sleep here if you like. The night is very cold. It's dangerous for a young man like you to be alone in this mist. Luiçiana Wood has more than trees and stones. Creatures. Tomorrow, at first light, I don't want to see you here. I've been kind enough."

"You don't understand, sir!"

"No! The one who doesn't understand is you, boy. Don't force me to kick you out right now. You wouldn't last a second out there. Believe me."

"The wolf, sir! The wolf! The wolf of White Cliffs! It's attacked again. It's in the hills of Constança Valley! The wolf brought tragedy. All over again."

I had to sit back down. That wasn't possible. No way. Not again. That was many years ago. Many. The wolf of White Cliffs had to be dead by now, unless it was a devil from hell. No way. Impossible. The boy put his hand in his jacket and pulled out a letter sealed with the Guimaraes' coat of arms. I stared at that piece of paper like a child. Then I took it in my hands. Opened the envelope slowly and removed the letter, the handwriting of which was careful and refined. The words seemed to have come straight from the Count's mouth. He wished to hire my services as a "wolf hunter". It seemed a wild animal had entered his dominions. To begin with, dead livestock. Sheep, the odd cow... Although there aren't usually wolf attacks in Constança Valley, it's frequent to come across wild dogs that have attacked a shepherd and his flock. That might have been normal, were it not for...

"The Count's son," said the boy. "The Count's son turned up dead. His entrails devoured. He was just a boy. Like in White Cliffs. My lord is prepared to pay whatever it takes for you to come to the Valley in search of that devilish beast. This is an advance."

Johan unhooked a bag he was carrying inside his trousers and tossed it at my feet. The bag fell open, and out came twenty or thirty gold coins engraved with the *Queen's* image. They shone on the floor like small suns in a darkness sent to sleep by the Count's letter.

"When the work is done, you'll receive another bag with the same coins. A good retirement plan, Mr d'Ourantes."

I examined the scattered coins. The fire that was about to go out. The fire. Heard the shouts. The shouts. Once again. Inside my head. I watched them. I examined the night through the window. Examined myself, outside in. Inside out. My own blackness.

"You know I never managed to hunt down the wolf of White Cliffs."

"Yes. But I also know you're the best hunter there is. If you can't, who will? It's a good chance to settle that business from White Cliffs. The Count trusts you, sir. The whole Valley trusts you."

"You're wrong about one thing. There is no settling that business from White Cliffs."

## WE ARE THE BIRDS THAT STAY

The trip lasts seven days. Seven wintry days to Constança Valley. Johan Pelaiz had everything ready to return to his lord's lands. But I didn't like the idea of a fixed route. There are lots of people in the wood who await the return journey. Bandits. Thieves. Rapists. On the outward journey, they watch you through the undergrowth and trees. Analyze your movement. Memorize your footsteps. Gestures. On the return journey is when they act. Rob. Beat. Strip you of all your possessions. Of your dignity, even. That's why I decided not to go back the same way. Johan didn't approve of my decision. But he had to put up with it and obey, because if he wanted me to go with him, then he had no choice.

I opened my old wooden trunk. A space that contains only memories. Took out the clothes I used to hunt wolves. My mourning clothes. Black. Black as the depths they were kept in. I put a piece of rope and a woollen blanket in a leather bag.

"Is that all you're taking?"

"What else should I take?" I answered the boy.

"Wolf hunters have certain... certain tools to trap the animal, don't they?"

"Other hunters, yes. I just need this," I pointed to my forehead. "And this," I showed him my knife.

We left for the Valley with the *bare minimum*. We needed to travel light and quickly. Barely stopping. We rode for two days beneath a sky on the verge of tears and an empty night of moon and stars. The third day, we turned off the road to rest at Souls' Inn, in the village of Cold Fountain. The horses needed to catch their breath. So did we. Souls' Inn is always full of suspicious-looking men. That said, nobody asks questions, everyone minds their own business. It's a discreet place for those who wish to pass unnoticed. That was the intention – to pass unnoticed. To be invisible.

We sat at a table and ordered a jug of wine with two bowls. Meanwhile, the owner's wife prepared a room lit by a candle, with two mattresses stuffed with straw and chicken feathers.

"So, where did you fight?" I asked the boy.

"You what? Fight?"

"That's right. You said you were in the *Queen's* troops. Where?"

Johan took a swig from his bowl and then sighed. He wiped the sweat pouring off his forehead with the sleeve of his shirt. There was a real ruckus going on in the inn. Men talking out loud and shouting. Banging the tables. Tossing wine on the bare floor. Cursing. Johan Pelaiz looked around and felt small in that chaotic, imperfect universe.

"The truth is I never went to war," he said, his voice hanging by a thread. "I lied to you. Ex... excuse me. I... I was just carrying out orders. Just orders. Nothing else. I wanted to embark on the ships of our *Queen's* navy, but my father suffers from a very serious illness. Very serious. It's just the two of us. My mother died of influenza three years ago. Ever since, my father has been fading from this world. He's blind. Lame in one leg. The only thing he does is pray to *God* to take him as soon as possible."

Johan lowered his head and took another swig of wine. This time, it was a long swig – the last before he left everything behind. Absolutely everything. His father. The memory of his mother. The last remnant of life. The last drop of blood. He was a wretched child. That much was clear to see. He had a sad expression, wrinkled by a blazing fire. Fire. Always.

"No need to apologize. I knew anyway. You've never witnessed war. You haven't seen bodies opened with all the shit we carry inside coming out. Or amputated corpses. The explosions of cannons. You haven't seen men screaming like children. The pain. The blade of a sword piercing flesh. No. You've never seen that. I knew it as soon as you set foot inside my house and I looked in your eyes. It's something I learnt to do in the *jungle*.

It's something *they* taught me. How to read people as if they were a book that contains a more or less interesting story. Your story strikes me as boring. No intrigue. A simple life, in a simple place. A boy like you should try emotion. Put your feelings out there for all to see. As much as possible. Fall in love. Almost lose your life. Step in enemy territory. Eat disgusting things. Go hungry. Drink the blood of a camel. Take a life. Pardon a life. Have the blade of a knife on your neck. Watch a friend die and be unable to do anything. Shout with rage. Make love to a native. Have a child. Walk naked in the *jungle*. Speak another language."

The fights started in the inn. The night brought with it the release of those who came with the intention of kicking up a fuss. We didn't want problems. Sometimes coming across problems is inevitable. Most of all because one doesn't go looking for problems, but they come looking for you. That's how it is. A natural law.

Two men were brawling. One was tall and strong. Bald and long-nosed. He was called the Hammer. Apparently he was the blacksmith in Cold Fountain, a quiet man weighing in at a hundred kilos or more who needed to let off steam with a few wines and the interpretation of a bad look on the part of some stranger. His rival was spending his first night at the inn. Nobody knew him. He was small, thin, and agile. He knew very well what he was doing, so much so that he landed the Hammer on the floor with just three blows. Everybody watched on in amazement. Nobody in Cold Fountain was capable of flooring the blacksmith. The

Hammer wanted to get up to carry on fighting. That moment when the mind is willing, but the body is ruled by physics and can't. No. It can't. Impossible for flesh and bones to endure all that wear and tear. The stranger glared at the Hammer and warned him to stay where he was. Pointed with his finger. The Hammer was coming out with incomprehensible words. Nobody knew why the fight had started. It's normally for some absurd reason. Something the protagonists cannot recall once it's over. Perhaps the Hammer had made some snide remark regarding the stranger's low stature. Or perhaps the aforementioned stranger had insinuated that the Hammer was fat, hairless, poorly endowed. To question a man's virility is always offensive. What was clear was that this stranger knew how to move and fight, something difficult to come across in these parts. Men launch their fists into the air without logic. Sometimes it seems they're fighting spirits only they can see. What was clear was that Souls' Inn was not the right place to pass unnoticed; it seemed to be a village tavern where men argue, shout, bang the tables, and fight until they bleed. Then they go home and do more of the same.

We went to our room. Our idea was to sleep for four or five hours and leave at first light to reach Minho Dock and take a boat down to Royal Thorn County. Once there, we would have to walk the narrow path that crosses Moor's Peak, in order then to descend again to the thickness of Touxido dry wood, which precedes the green borders of Constança Valley. It's a long road. It's a hard road. Sharp stones. The river. Steep slopes. Cliffs. Gorse. Wild animals. Thieves.

I lay on the floor with an old, yellow pillow propped beneath my neck. The boy looked at me from one of the beds, unable to comprehend this movement. He scratched his head, covered himself up to his neck, and insisted once more.

"Wouldn't it be better to sleep in the bed, sir? It isn't very comfortable, but I suppose it's better than sleeping on the stone floor."

"Go to sleep, boy. You're going to need it. Tomorrow will be a long day. Very long. Make the most of it. The night in Cold Fountain is silent. There are no sounds. No little owls. The trees stop and turn to stone. The wolf takes refuge in damp caves. The water of the streams returns to the source, moving slowly like a snake. The night is a painting in which it's difficult to make out objects. Go to sleep."

Johan Pelaiz sighed and looked at me again from the bed. This time, his face showed indifference. He raised his eyebrows and turned towards the wall.

"Yes, it would be better to have a little sleep. You should sleep as well. It seems the wine has affected your good judgement," he murmured.

In the *jungle*, we slept on the damp floor. The *jungle* floor is always damp. In the morning, you might come across a snake at your feet, or a tarantula ruffling your hair. Somebody might turn up dead because of an insect bite or something. Nocturnal animals won't do anything to you if you're not afraid. I wasn't afraid. Not of them. Other animals are worse. Nocturnal and daytime. Those that walk on two legs and carry a musket on their back. A machete. A sword. A knife. Kill for pleasure. Rape the natives. Mistreat. Raise flags in the name of some *King* or the Church. We are worse. I'm aware I cannot solve the atrocities I have committed with my own two hands. I am guilty for my actions. Beyond forgiveness.

When Johan opened his eyes, on account of the gentle clarity seeping through the window, I was already downstairs, getting the horses ready to leave Cold Fountain as quickly as possible. It seemed we were the first to get up. Not a sound came from inside the inn. Outside, the wood had woken already and was letting its melody flow through the gaps in the trees.

"Excuse me, sir. I didn't have a very good night."

"I know, boy. You were tossing and turning. Who's Aloia? You kept on saying that name. Aloia, Aloia, Aloia..."

Johan Pelaiz stared at me. His cheeks turned red. He readjusted the saddle on his horse. Passed his hand over the horse's back. Softly. Then got on.

"A girl."

"Yes, I imagined as much."

"She's the Count's daughter, sir."

"The Count? The Count of Constança?"

"That's right, sir. I've known her since we were children. We're close friends. Or at least we were. Now... Now, I don't know anything about her."

Johan directed his horse towards the start of the road. A road that seemed pleasant and simple, but would soon become dark and dangerous. Meandering. Going up and down. Up again. An overwhelming road. Vomit-inducing. Exhausting. He already had Aloia's image on his mind. A memory had returned. Whatever it was. I wasn't interested. We had to have our five senses focused on the journey. There would be time later to rummage in our sufferings. There's always time for that. To be tormented.

We reached Minho Dock almost without obstacles. Johan had been complaining about a bee sting that had caused a red lump on his neck. I warned him not to scratch it. He ignored me. We barely said a word the whole way. I don't like talking on such long journeys. I am unfamiliar with the route and don't even trust the wind sifting through the branches of the trees. Sometimes, even here, things are not what they seem.

In the Dock, two boats were tied up. The river was swollen. It hadn't stopped raining in weeks, although not a single drop had fallen the last few days. Even so, the sky was always threatening to shed the odd tear.

"Good morning to you, gentlemen," said the old man in charge of the boats. "What can I do for you?"

He looked unkempt. Lacking a left eye. The wound was open. I didn't mind. I've seen worse things. He had a grey beard that covered his neck. He came over, leaning on a carefully crafted stick.

"Good morning to you too. We would like to go down the river to Royal Thorn Dock."

"Ahhh... It seems everybody's going to Royal Thorn. Just now, I rented a boat to a small man with a foreign accent. Or at least that's what I thought. This hasn't been working properly for a while," he said, pointing to his ear. "Are you after the reward as well?"

"What reward?"

"Don't you know? The lord of Thorn is offering a thousand coins for the head of the Thorn Fox."

"The Thorn Fox?"

"Tirso Migues, sir. The Thorn Fox."

"And what did the Thorn Fox do for his lord to offer such a large amount?"

The old man started laughing so much he almost let go of the stick and fell flat on his face. That didn't happen. He took out a dirty handkerchief and blew his nose hard. Put it back in his pocket. His smile still hanging there, he wiped away the saliva that had accumulated at the corners of winter-chapped lips.

"Forgive me... Forgive me, sir. I wasn't laughing at you. No, I wasn't."

"Then who were you laughing at?" I asked with raised eyebrows.

"Your question. That's right. Your question. Why do you think the lord of Royal Thorn would offer a thousand gold coins? Because they were stolen from him! That's right! Stolen! By the Fox! You know these are troubled times we live in. There's a revolt on the way. Another revolt. Like the one we can't talk about. The one we're not allowed even to mention. People don't forget. Remember, 'The sparrows will run after the falcons.'"

Another revolt. It's forbidden to talk about that. It's forbidden to say that sentence. "The sparrows will run after the falcons." Were one of the *Queen's* spies to hear him, they would cut off the old man's head. A long time ago. So far away it reached us in the form of a legend. It wasn't a legend. It was true. My grandfather told me. He heard it from his grandfather, who heard it from his grandfather as well. It was like a secret you inherited so nobody would forget what had happened centuries earlier. An atrocity. Death. Civil war.

"I don't care what this Tirso gets up to… The Fox, as you call him. We're not even going to spend a day in Thorn County. We just want to travel downriver. Please rent us a boat."

The old man looked me up and down and said something under his breath. It may have been nothing. One of those murmurs of distrust or doubt. "Mmmmmmmmm…" He gestured towards me with his stick.

"Pardon me, sir. Can you tell me your name?"

"Not if you don't tell me yours first. One needs to know who one is talking to."

The old man mumbled again. Leant heavily on his stick. Raised his head and stroked his long beard. Took two steps forwards and stood right in front of my nose.

"I'm One-Eyed Martiño. I don't much like the description. One-Eyed. It sounds disrespectful to me. Like I was no good. I lost that eye fighting for my *King*. Fighting for all of you. And what do I have now? You can see. I have nothing. Nothing. A boat that barely provides me with a living. A house made of four planks. The wooden cross with my wife's body. A son at the bottom of the sea, in the remains of a ship from the navy. Four onions planted in my vegetable garden. A hen that can't lay eggs. And solitude waiting for me by the fire."

"Well, that's more than I have," I remarked.

The old man gazed at me with barely suppressed rage. Then he burst out laughing. This time, he was unable to stay on his feet and collapsed on the ground. He wanted to get up, but couldn't and held out a hand for us to help him. Johan went over and lifted him to his feet. The old man grabbed the stick and leant on it, as if seeking a moment's respite.

"Fair enough. You can always find someone who's worse off than you. That's true. Really true. You still haven't told me your name. No name, no boat."

"Lourenço d'Ourantes."

"D'Ourantes?" repeated One-Eyed Martiño. "D'Ourantes, d'Ourantes, d'Ourantes... I heard of a d'Ourantes way back. He used to hunt wolves. They say he was the best. They also said he was a bit crazy. You know what tongues are like. Apparently he used to talk to trees and stuff like that. To animals. The earth. What nonsense. *God* take me if that's not what I heard. That's right. That's what passers-by told me. Can you believe it? With his hands! He used to hunt wolves with his hands!"

"People have a vivid imagination."

"Yes, they do. I don't suppose it's you. This d'Ourantes... No, impossible. It was a long time ago. He must be more than dead by now."

"Are you going to rent me a boat, or not?"

The old man looked up at the sky and turned around. He walked towards one of the moored boats. Gestured to us to come over.

"Hurry! It's going to rain! There's still a way to go before you reach Thorn Dock. It's dangerous taking horses on a boat like this. But the river is calm today. Be careful now."

We paid One-Eyed Martiño for the hire of the boat. It was a square, stable boat. Made of solid wood. We had to push with a pole that touched the muddy bottom of the river. Johan looked ahead attentively. I tried to do the same, but the truth is the water of the river fills me with respect. And nervousness. In the *jungle*, the river carried strange creatures. Whenever we crossed it, with the water up to our necks, people were suddenly swept into its depths. We never saw them again. The natives said it was mermaids swimming upriver from the sea who had a taste for fresh water and fish. A taste for handsome, young men, more like. I never paid them all that much attention, but the natives were rarely or never wrong.

# A WOUNDED DEER LEAPS HIGHEST

Thorn Dock was deserted. Five boats had been moored up. We did the same with ours. We could see the town of Royal Thorn from the river. A grey mirage consisting of houses and stone walls. Above it, hugging the county in an embrace, the bare mountain of Moor's Peak.

Royal Thorn is known for its quarries. Most of the *Kingdom's* cathedrals were built with stone from here. In fact, part of the quarries belongs to the Church.

We rode quickly to the entrance of the town. Found nobody along the way. That was strange. Thorn has a certain amount of commercial activity. The market was empty of stalls and people planning to buy or make an exchange. Johan pointed to an old man sitting on the steps in front of some house. We went over to him without getting off our horses.

"Good day, old man."

The old man lifted his head. He had long, white hair and bandaged eyes. Between his bare feet, which were covered in sores, with rotten nails, was a worn wooden bowl with nothing in it.

"A coin, sir. A coin for this poor blind man. A coin to buy something to put in his mouth," he begged.

I gestured to Johan to give him alms. The boy looked at me in surprise, with raised eyebrows. I don't know whether it was because he hadn't understood my mute message or because he refused to give a coin to this poor old man who was up to his ears in shit.

"My lord said the money…"

"Your lord can say whatever he likes," I interrupted the boy. "You want me to go with you, right? Then give the old man a coin."

Johan Pelaiz pulled out the bag hidden in his trousers. Got off his horse and carefully placed a coin in the bottom of that bowl that was as old as its owner. The old man bowed his head in gratitude.

"Thank you, sirs. May *God* bless you."

"Forgive me. We've just arrived in Thorn and…"

"I know. You're not from these parts. It's pretty obvious."

"How come?"

The old man let out a smile. It seemed he hadn't smiled in ages. Hadn't stretched his lips. Like it was the memory of better times. He scratched the wound on his left elbow. Wiped his hands on the sheet that was his clothing. A sheet that was torn in hundreds of places and reached down to his bare knees.

"The good thing about being blind is the other senses get sharper, you see? Your accent gives you away. You're from further up there," he lifted his thumb and pointed at the sky. "From the north."

"Right...Not that high, I hope," I said a little ironically. "The fact is the streets are deserted, and that's not normal for a place that is sometimes very busy. Where is everybody?"

"Don't you know? They caught the Fox! He was captured this morning. Everybody's gone there."

"There? Where?"

"The Count's palace. He's going to be paraded like a trophy. A boar's head. Lots of people don't like it. Lots of people love the Fox, you see? The Fox would share out whatever he stole among the poor. And we're almost all poor around here. They're furious. For them, the Thorn Fox is a blessing from *God*."

There was no point stopping. No point sticking our noses in at the Count's palace. If the Fox had been captured, that wasn't our problem. We had to head quickly to the Valley. Perhaps this suited us. Everyone had gathered at the palace gates. That was good. We could pass unnoticed. To pass unnoticed is good. Fewer problems.

The rays broke through the cloudy sky and beat against the polished, white stones of Moor's Peak. The day lit up in a second. In the twinkling of an eye. An instant. Look behind on hearing an unfamiliar sound.

An outbreath caused by tiredness. Death. Then back to a gloomy landscape. Shadows on the landscape.

Moor's Pass is a stone road that sinks into the mountain and climbs again. And so on until it reaches the borders of Touxido dry wood. It's all stones and the skeletons of deceased nature. In the old days, Moor's Peak was known as Thick Cork. A mountainous tongue full of tall trees and steep vegetation. When the Moorish general Kamra reached the mountain with her troops, she decided to burn it. Kamra, nicknamed Fire Moon, was in the habit of attacking at night, and Thick Cork didn't let her see the sky. She couldn't discern the stars. The constellations. The moon. They say she got undressed and merged with the nocturnal animals. Turned into a white wolf and ran among the trees. Along the paths. Drank the water of pools and rivers. Climbed the peak and howled in the depths of the wood. Then destroyed everything.

Moor's Peak does your feet in. Makes them bloody. The horses have a hard time of it as well. They fall to the ground when they step on loose stones. Slip as they're descending. Slip as they're ascending.

"Water, sir. A sip of water," pleaded Johan.

"We can't, boy. Not yet. We have to get through this bit as quickly as possible. We have to reach Moor's Rest. There's a grass clearing there with trees and a little stream. Not far to go now."

"But I'm dying of thirst, milord. Just a tiny sip. The horses could do with one as well."

"I said no. We have to get to the Rest. We'll take a break once we get there."

I could feel the horse's breath on the back of my neck. It was warm and dry. A last sigh before the end. I also needed water. Even so, I tried not to think about it. To divert my attention. At times like this, I am inevitably reminded of the *jungle*. Humidity. Snakes at my feet. Mutilated bodies. Pale bodies. The *jungle's* embrace has nothing to do with Moor's Peak. Moor's Peak is a stone corpse with a beginning and an end. It's all marked out. The *jungle* has its own life. It's a mother who does everything to protect her children. Protects them with all she has. It's a maze that erodes the senses. You don't know where you are. You get lost. A compass won't help you. The *jungle* is a box of surprises. Men start seeing images that exist only in their imagination. Illusions. They become violent and deranged. Two days later, they turn up dead, killed by the poisonous dart of some tribe. Or beheaded. That's right. There were lots of beheadings. That's a quick death. We didn't deserve a quick death. We deserved a slow death. Bloody. Very bloody. Painful.

From the road, we could hear the little stream of Moor's Rest in the distance. Johan, who was walking as if he had no soul, ran towards the clearing. Along the way, he tripped a couple of times on the stones. He got up and carried on running, impelled by the urgent need to drink. His elbows and knees were bloody. The image of a clean, impeccable boy he'd shown the first time he knocked at my door was nothing but a mirage.

"All right, boy. Drink slowly. You'll do yourself some harm."

Johan stuck his head in the stream. Washed his face with the water. Lay on the grass with open hands, as if seeking a ray of serenity. The heat of the sun. His breathing was ragged. He opened his eyes and stared at a bird on the branch of an oak.

"This is the road to hell, milord."

"This is the road to Constança Valley. Is the Valley hell?" I smiled.

"We had to take the same route back. I didn't have any problems when I went to fetch you from Luiçiana. The journey takes two days longer. That's true. But it's all much easier, sir."

"Don't make me say it again, boy. The road through St Stephen is dangerous. There are invisible eyes that watch you on the outward journey. On the way back…"

Suddenly the blade of a knife pressed against my throat. A cold, revolting touch. It wasn't the first time. Nor will it be the last, I suppose. Johan felt the circumference of a musket on the back of his neck. For him, it was the first time. Two more men came up behind me. I could hear their footsteps on the grass. Another two took up position behind the boy. I saw them with my own eyes. They struck me on the legs. I knelt down. A well-intoned song came towards us from the vegetation.

"'I felt the knife piercing my chest. I heard my lover crying ouuuuuuut… I felt my heart beating like crazy. I heard my son weeeeeeeeping… Ah, my love, so near and yet so far, war is hell…' Well, good morning, gentlemen," I could see the stranger's feet right in front of me. "It's a lovely day, isn't it?"

"I can't appreciate it from here quite as much as I would like," I complained.

"Lift him up."

The knife disappeared from my throat. Two men grabbed me by the arms and stood me on my feet. I tried to envisage my surroundings. Make calculations. How many men were there? How many of them were armed? How were they built? What were my options? That's why, to start with, I let myself go. I need time to analyze the situation. To calculate. Then I hatch a plan inside my head. After that, I risk putting it into action.

The stranger was a tall, slim man. He had just shaved. He had a musket hanging off his back and an enormous knife on the side of his belt. He was wearing a yellowish shirt, which was half unbuttoned. His trousers were leather. He had a snake tattooed on his left arm. It went down from his shoulder and ended with an open mouth at his wrist.

One of the men standing there went over to the stranger and whispered something in his ear. He opened his eyes wide and turned around. He gestured with his head for them to lift Johan. The boy was frightened. He started praying under his breath. We could all hear his supplications.

"You!" barked the stranger. "What's your name?"

"Jo... Johan. Johan Pelaiz, sir. From Constança Valley, sir."

One of the men holding Johan started frisking him with a certain sensuality. First, his shirt. Down to his trousers. Then his boots. All very slowly and methodically. Lingering over each piece of cloth he touched. The man was wearing a huge hat and a scarf that almost covered his whole face. Only his eyes were visible. These enormous green eyes. Round. It was then I knew this wasn't a man, but a woman.

After the sensual search, she took out the coins Johan kept in his pocket. She wasn't happy with the end result. She shook her head at the stranger, who appeared to be the leader of that band of *highwaymen*. In another mute gesture, he lifted his chin and raised his arms, as if demanding an explanation. He turned around. Walked towards Johan. Stopped.

"Where is it?"

"Where is... what?"

"You know what."

"No, I don't, sir," replied the boy fearfully.

"Little Owl!" shouted the stranger. "Remind Mr Pelaiz, son of Constança Valley, what it is we need so he can go back to his lord's lands."

Little Owl was a fat, hairy guy dressed in a suit of armour made of bark. It was obvious at first sight that his head didn't work very well. I don't just mean the left eye that wandered at will. His physiognomy seemed to imply a certain backwardness. The way he stuck his finger in his mouth. The way he swayed when he walked. The difficulty with his tongue when he tried to pronounce words. In Luiçiana, there's an old man in the mountains who lives in Suebian Cave, a cave dug out of the rock that served as a refuge for shepherds before old Milíades began to use it as a residence. Every day of the week, Milíades is a different person, animal, or thing. An English king, a bird, a solder who's just come back from war, a sailor, a tree... Little Owl reminded me of old, crazy Milíades, who seemed to have been wandering the mountains of Luiçiana for more than a thousand years.

"A... a... a... mmmmmmm... ba... ba... bag... fu... fu... full... mmmmmm... of... mmmmmmm... co... co... co... coins."

"You see? Even Little Owl knows why you've been arrested, Mr Pelaiz. You travelled on the St Stephen road, didn't you?"

Johan nodded timidly.

"And you were carrying a bag full of coins, weren't you?" continued the stranger.

Johan lifted his eyes. Looked at me. He tried to do it without being noticed, but didn't succeed. The stranger followed the invisible line that a look leaves in its wake. Swivelled around. Walked towards me.

"Search this one," he ordered.

The woman hiding behind a hat and scarf came over. Ran her soft hands over my body. I lifted my arms as if surrendering to the enemy. Kept my eyes on her. She kept her eyes on me. She was young. Pretty. Smelled of strawberries. I liked her. She started getting nervous. She had a knife loosely tucked into her trousers. She sighed. I sighed. She looked up again. Stopped. I winked at her. Quickly took out the knife and placed it against her throat. She shouted. The hat fell to the ground, and a long mane of blond, curly hair burst into the air. Johan opened his eyes wide, hypnotized by this celestial image. Everybody grabbed their musket and aimed their barrel at me.

"Right," I said. "Here's the deal. We continue on our way. You continue on yours. Nobody gets wounded."

"Let go of the knife if you do not want to die," hissed the stranger.

The men walked slowly towards me. There were eight of them. I pressed the knife harder against the girl's throat. She cried out. The stranger raised a hand as if wanting to stop me from a distance. But what he actually wanted was to stop his comrades in their tracks.

"Well, now! It seems the girl is worth more than it appears. Mmmmmmm... let me think. She's your daughter, right? Of course! She has the same nose as her father," I replied, gazing at the stranger. "I suppose your eyes are your mother's," I whispered mockingly in her ear.

"I don't think you realize what you're getting into. Do you know who I am? Do you know who we are?"

"Enlighten me, please."

The stranger turned around and stared into the depths of that small wood situated by *God* on the rocky slopes of Moor's Peak. A snippet of hope. A refuge. The perfect proof that even in hell there's a pleasant place in which to rest.

"We are the Thorn Animals. Those who seek justice for ordinary people. The one talking to you is Tirso Migues, the Fox."

"If you're the Fox, who's on the way to the gallows in the Count of Thorn's palace?"

Tirso turned around. Walked with his hands behind his back.

"A brave man who is aware of our cause."

"A brave man? If he's the brave man, then what are you? The coward?"

The Fox raised his hand and shouted in a fury.

"You don't understand! The cause comes first. There are times sacrifices require a life. We all know that. Snake understood that. That's why he volunteered to stand in for me. Because, behind all of this, there's a plan. A plan the Count is not expecting. That will be when we avenge Snake's death. And now, do me a favour and hand over my daughter."

The Fox placed his barrel on Johan Pelaiz's head. The boy deposited an air of lament on the grass. Grabbed a handful of earth as if clinging to this world before passing to the next. Before hearing the final boom!

"Let us leave. Nobody gets hurt."

"I can't. You've seen me now. I can't let you go. Let go of her, or I'll kill him right away," he pressed the barrel into Johan's hair.

"Do that, and she'll have no neck," I warned him.

At this moment of agonizing tension – not comparable to the numerous times I have been on the verge of dying in more painful, horrifying ways – a gentle breeze stirred the grass of Moor's Rest. Stirred the trees. Stirred the gorse. Stirred all those insects that might have been in their habitat. Stirred all of us. Even so, this virtually divine instant did not restore sanity to either side of the conflict.

"Who is he?" the Fox asked Johan while pressing the barrel against his forehead.

"I... I... I..." said the boy on the verge of tears.

"Who the hell is he?" shouted the Fox.

"Captain Lourenço d'Ourantes, sir!"

I closed my eyes. I was sorry Johan had said my name. You never know who you're going to meet. The past follows you like a son. I had a son. Not anymore. The Fox stared at me. In amazement. Lowered his barrel and aimed it at the ground. Johan breathed a sigh of relief on seeing this gesture that could have been the start of getting out of there alive.

"Lourenço d'Ourantes? The wolf hunter? Impossible."

The Fox came towards me. His eyes were wrinkled as if seeking to recognize me in a past meeting I didn't remember.

"I was there," he continued. "I was there. In White Cliffs. You saved me from the wolf. I was a boy, a child… But… No… It's impossible. You'd have to be an old man… You'd have to have… To be… It seems the years stopped passing for you, sir. Impossible. A witch's enchantment."

The Fox ordered his men to lower their muskets. I did the same and let go of the knife. The girl ran into her father's arms. They gave each other a long, sentimental hug. Johan's heart was pounding furiously. Boom boom boom boom boom boom boom! I could hear it from where I was standing. I don't know if it was because of those agonizing minutes when his life was hanging by a trigger or from seeing the girl's figure again, albeit briefly and hurriedly. I think it must have been the latter.

"I remember you," I said. "Of course! Migues. You were the son of Afonço Migues, White Cliffs' tavern-keeper."

"I owe you my life, sir. Were it not for you, I'd have died with the others in that accursed field. Forgive me.

I... I didn't know. I still can't quite believe it. It seems I have more wrinkles than you. It seems you made a pact with the devil."

The Fox offered us a plate of hot food. We didn't say no. They blindfolded us to take us to their refuge. It was a pointless act. When you survive the *jungle*, you learn a lot of things. All those years... Knowing how to orient yourself is essential. You have to interpret the forest. The way. The stones. The stream. The wind. The leaves of the trees. I was fully aware where they were taking us. The next day, I could have gone to the Thorn Count's palace and handed over the information for a large number of coins. But I wouldn't.

Night became night. All so slowly we didn't even realize it had happened. The Fox had a well-ordered refuge. There were huts in the treetops and wooden walkways going from one to the next. Anyone who understands a bit about tactics knows height is always an advantage.

They lit some fires. The women prepared dinner. The men drank. There were hens and pigs. The odd dog. We sat on a trunk next to the fire. The Fox brought me a glass of wine and a chicken leg. Truth is I was hungry. Johan ate as if this was his last day on earth. The moon was nowhere to be seen. Yet again. It doesn't show itself here, like in Luiçiana. And when it peeps through the clouds, strange creatures emerge in the wood.

"Is it good?"

"What?" I asked in return.

"The wine! It comes straight from the Count's cellars. He imports twenty-five barrels every year from

France. On the last trip, they didn't all make it to their destination," he grinned.

"I can imagine. You should be careful. Moor's Rest is not the best place to hide out."

"This is just one of many refuges we have. The Count's stay in these lands will soon come to an end."

"If there's something I've learnt in this life, it's never underestimate the powerful. Money doesn't guarantee intelligence, but it does buy men. Friends quickly become enemies with a few coins."

A little owl watched us indifferently from a tree. It was in its habitat. It was part of a muffled landscape. At first light, it will go back to where it came from. It seemed the wood was writhing about while the moon illuminated all those places in the world that had a spark of hope in them. Here there was no hope, only darkness and grief.

We had to rest. We had one last bit to get to the Valley. A hard, dangerous road like Moor's Pass. Johan tossed and turned and talked under his breath. Sweated. I suppose he hadn't got over the fright. Or he was dreaming of the Fox's daughter. She went over to him and wiped his forehead with a cloth. He opened his eyes and went red. They gazed at each other. Looks that carry invisible messages. The Fox's daughter walked slowly into the wood. Johan watched as the girl's figure was swallowed up by the darkness. And his heart stopped for a moment. A tiny moment. A knife rummaged in his insides. He loved her. He knew the meaning of that word. Then he remembered the Count of Constança's daughter. Aloia was her name. He lay back on the ground. Tried to sleep, even though he wouldn't get any rest the whole night. Love. Or the illusion of something that might be love. It's that simple.

"Why are you going to Constança Valley?" asked the Fox.

"Wolves."

"I heard you'd given up that profession after the business in White Cliffs."

"You heard correctly."

"So?"

"So... It might be the same wolf. Not the same physically. That's impossible. It was a long time ago. But evil is inherited. Inherited... And this wolf... I don't know. There's something pushing me to go."

The Fox fell silent for a moment. Moved one of the sticks burning in the fire.

"And what's that?" he asked, illuminated by the fire.

"It killed a child. The Count's son. A boy who was only just eight."

He lowered his head.

"Like in White Cliffs," he observed.

# THE SMITTEN ROCK THAT GUSHES

Touxido dry wood. It's not actually all that dry. It's a dead wood that preserves a certain dark greenness. It's a ghost that arose on the ancient lagoon of Touxido. It's full of the corpses of animals that drank from its poisoned waters. Only those that knew how to adapt to its environment survived. St Martin's *black frogs*. They're small. As small as a toenail. They get inside the orifices of living creatures. Lay their eggs there. Inside. Deep down. The *goblin*, a rat the size of a cat. It digs tunnels beneath the muddy earth. You have to be careful where you step. The *láncara*, a fish that is like a snake. Green with misshapen black spots on its back. It has long, sharp teeth. It can snap off your leg with a single bite. More and more animals. All dark.

Mysterious. Horrifying. Touxido dry wood is a piece of the *jungle* in these muffled lands.

Everything has its story. This place as well. There used to be a large castro settlement here. A city which – people say as one of those legends that travel from mouth to mouth – was the largest in the north. Active and trading. *Béal Spéir* according to the castro dwellers. *Lacus Glaciem* to the Romans.

Nihme is a figure they use to frighten children in these parts. "Nihme will come, and the water will be poisoned." He's a large, strong man dressed in metal and a long red cape that hangs off his shoulders. He wears a helmet in which he hides his snakelike eyes. The fact is the figure of Nihme came about because of a legend about Roman troops arriving in *Béal Spéir*. A Roman general, whose name has been lost behind Nihme's apparent monstrosity, came to conquer this land for the greater glory of the Empire. He promised Caesar he would subject the barbarian peoples without spilling a drop of Roman blood. He negotiated with the leaders of each tribe so they would accept his military superiority and the Empire's power peacefully. Sometimes this self-confident bureaucracy worked. Others, it didn't. When that happened, Nihme sought out alternative methods. He would cut off the leaders' heads in front of the whole community, surround the villages, burn the livestock and crops... all so that those who opposed being conquered would reconsider their decision. *Pax*. The winter was cold when Nihme reached the gates of *Béal Spéir*. Snow covered the road, and the lake was frozen. The general was amazed at this stone city with its narrow streets and thick, high wall. As the good soldier he was, he knew conquest would be difficult. They had no advantage over the camp's fortifications. If they did get inside the city, the narrow, winding streets could turn into a real massacre for his troops.

*Ceann Loch* was a shrewd leader. He refused the agreement the Roman general offered him. He was aware of *Béal Spéir's* advantages. Also, he had men who knew how to fight, and the women were well-trained archers. The Roman general withdrew his troops to the forest and waited for winter to pass. A snowy winter. Ice. Cold. Death. Many were buried beneath that icy land. And yet the general stood firm. He didn't budge from the front at *Béal Spéir*. He devised a plan. He watched them patiently. How they moved. How they fed themselves. What life was like day by day in the city. He sent soldiers in plain clothes who informed Nihme about movements in the city. And one morning, watching through the trees, he saw there was a hole on one side of *Béal Spéir* where the water from the lake went in. His spies told him this opening was just the start of a tunnel that carried water to a large open-air well inside the city. There, every morning, the women would go in search of water for their livestock and families. It was then the general came up with an idea to put an end to this wait that was costing the sons of Rome dear. So Nihme acted like his namesake and poisoned all the water in the lake. In two weeks, *Béal Spéir* fell to the Roman sword, and the corpses, many of which were decomposed, were thrown into the lake.

Hundreds of years later, this is the result. The landscape has become twisted because of the poison.

The wood rotted, and now everything looks like a swamp full of inhospitable creatures. You have to be very careful where you put your feet, because Touxido dry wood is full of mud and sand pits that swallow you up in the twinkling of an eye. You can't drink from the puddles of water. The poison is still there. The air is acidic. It makes sense to wear a scarf over your mouth.

"Is this the first time you've been to the dry wood?" I asked Johan.

"No, sir," he said with a look of disgust. "When I was ten, I went with my uncle to trade in Royal Thorn."

"I wouldn't have thought it's a good idea to bring a boy of that age to these parts."

"My uncle was very familiar with the roads, lord. And the passage through the dry wood was his favourite to get to Thorn. He said with a bit of a luck you wouldn't meet anybody on the way. He knew where to put his feet. He had these marks."

"Marks?"

"Yes, sir. He had memorized these marks. He knew from one point to another there was a mud pit, from here to there was a puddle whose water you could drink."

"Wow! I wouldn't mind having that information now."

"Don't worry. I'm also pretty familiar with these..."

Suddenly Johan was swallowed up by the earth. He had stepped right into a sand pit. The boy shouted and lifted his hands while sinking slowly. He came out with words like "Help me! *God*! Holy Victory of Constança!"

"Don't move! You'll only make it worse."

"Hurry up, milord!"

I went to get the rope I kept in my leather bag and tied one end to the horse's hip. I then threw the other end to Johan, who was now up to his chin in mud.

"Hold on tight!"

"I can't lift my arms! The... The sand is very heavy, sir! The devil is pulling me downwards! My *God*, save me from this imprudence!"

"Forget about the devil! Lift your arms! If you don't do that, you're going to drown in this mucky pit!"

Johan closed his eyes. Let out a cry of effort. I think it was effort. He managed to stick a hand in the air. The mud was already touching the tip of his long nose. I made the horse walk so it could pull on a sinking Johan. Little by little, the boy's body was raised to the surface by the horse's strength. He was breathing heavily as if wanting to come back to life. As if he'd been dead for a moment and *God* had waived the cost of the voyage.

"Thank you, Holy Victory of Constança. Thank you, my saint."

I raised my eyebrows. Went over to him. Wiped his face with a cloth. Placed my lips next to his ear.

"Don't mention it."

## TO FIGHT ALOUD IS VERY BRAVE

The Valley is green. Cold as well. It looks like a freshly cut pine coffin. The wood's new blood. Silence. Excessive. This wood is alive, but resentful. Angry. And the animals filter that desire for revenge. Feed on it. Hatred. They become more savage, more wild. Indomitable. The air is heavy and deep. As if it has been here since the beginning of everything. I don't like this place. It sends a shiver down my spine. Fear? No. The *jungle* gave me strength. There, I was afraid. There, emotions came out you only experience when you're a child and the world is a strange place you have to explore. There, I wished to die. Then I clung to life. Some time ago. A long time ago.

"What happened here, boy?"

"Where?"

"Where do you think? Here! In this wood!"

"Forgive me, milord. I haven't got over the fright. I almost…"

"Almost died," I interrupted him. "Now you have a story you can tell your grandchildren. So tell me, what was this place?"

Johan came alongside me. The horses were tired from a long journey and too many unforeseen circumstances. In the distance could be seen the end of the road from Touxido dry wood before you entered the Valley. A circle of light that seemed to suggest something better on the other side. A mirage. The Valley didn't have a very good reputation. Its peoples didn't want to go back to Constança. That was something that surprised me about Johan. As soon as his horse stepped into the entrance of the wood, he let out a delicate smile. As if he was now safe from all the dangers the road could provide. He was happy to be home, despite not appearing to be a very happy person. Around him, there was an aura of blackness and shame. He couldn't find a setting in a world constantly at war. He couldn't find himself. I know what that is.

"A place of sacrifice, sir. You know. People in the past. There are still lots of pagans living in the mountains. They worship ancient *Gods*. They don't accept the true faith."

I couldn't stop my insides churning. My whole body twisted and turned. Everything we carry inside. "The true faith." If I was paid a coin for every time I've heard that phrase, I'd be richer than any *King*. In the *jungle*, we had to show them the true faith. The true *God*. "You have to give them the true faith. To show them the true faith. With blood, they will accept the true faith."

The Gates of Holy Victory welcomed us with three hanging corpses. They swayed in this light, unpleasant breeze. Revolting. The bodies must have been there for several days. I didn't take my eyes off them. A father. A mother. A child. Dead. Johan didn't say anything. As if this was normal. He carried on with indifference, as we left behind that family hanging on three separate ropes. Rotting. I couldn't help taking one last look. I've seen more unpleasant things. That much is true. But seeing the child reminded me of Tarthai and the arrow sticking in his chest. I felt a shiver that slowly climbed my body.

"They're pagans, Mr d'Ourantes! An evil that still lurks in these lands!" shouted someone in front of me.

I turned my head towards Constança village. Three people on horseback awaited our presence as if they knew exactly what day and time we would arrive. Three people dressed like Johan in clothes that weren't from this century. The Valley's bishop was well turned out. He had a gold chain with a cross resting on his chest. He was a fat man, like all bishops. The man in the middle was Ricardo de Guimaraes, Count of Constança. He wore a long, bearskin coat. I didn't know who the third person was. I later found out he was called the Collector. He had a curly, chestnut-brown beard. He was tall. He didn't speak. Sometimes he would lift his upper lip and reveal a cynical smile and a gold tooth. He was the Count's right-hand man. I didn't take to him.

We rode slowly to the Count's palace. As we passed through Constança village, I barely saw anybody outside their houses. There was an older man cutting wood. As we passed next to him, he didn't even look up. A woman in dirty, torn clothes carried a basket of grass under her arm. She swayed her hips exaggeratedly. In one hand, she held a sickle. The muddy path stank of shit, and the mist cut the stone dwellings in half. Hens pecked at the ground. An aged dog lay waiting for death. Two cats fought on a rooftop. Apart from that, all was silence. Silence. A tragic atmosphere.

"You can see people are frightened. Misfortune brought fear to our beautiful county," said the bishop in a false tone of concern.

"Fear is part of our nature."

"Of *God's* nature, you mean. We are in his image and likeness."

"We heard you had one or two problems on the return journey," interjected the Count. "Though I suppose for a man of your reputation it was nothing compared to the lands of savages."

I wanted to think about my answer. I'm in a strange place, and you never know who might take offence at poorly considered words. And yet I couldn't help it.

"Believe me, Lord Count, when I tell you there are savages with more humanity than some Christians that step on this land."

The bishop's horse screeched to a halt. Drove its hooves into the mud. The other travellers – the Count, the Collector, and Johan – did the same.

"There are all kinds in the land of the *Lord*," the bishop continued this conversation that had every appearance of growing tense. "All the same, Mr d'Ourantes, we can't expect much from those who are unfamiliar with the Word of *God*, don't you think? I imagine you witnessed all manner of atrocities."

"Yes, sir. Like that of a child hanging next to its parents."

I stopped my horse with the image of the child etched on my brain and the sound of the rope still swaying in the distance. It was the image of the child, and at the same time the image of Tarthai looking at me. I hadn't had such visions for a while. Bits of reality that whizz past in front of me. Ta, ta, ta, ta, ta, ta, ta, ta... I hadn't recalled that moment for quite some time. I had the impression it was fading between memory and space, so I took a deep breath and endeavoured to come to. The bishop barely opened his eyes and carried on forwards. He let out a sigh of indifference.

"My dear sir, the devil can be found in the tiniest of bodies. Evil must be eradicated," he concluded.

The Collector came up behind me and gestured to me to continue. I obeyed, not wishing to debate Bishop del Riego's words. I was tired from the journey. Hungry and in need of a wash. Our arrival in Constança had been as expected. Cold. Hostile. And it didn't look like it was going to get any better.

## THE WIND BEGUN TO KNEAD THE GRASS

"Forgive my wife," repeated the Count. "She still hasn't got over the death of our son. It's all too recent. I pray to *God* to bring her back to us."

Amaina de Guimaraes threw herself at my feet in tears. She shouted to the sky for me to capture that "hellish demon" that had carried off her child. She tore her red linen dress. Tugged at her swarthy hair. Kissed my muddy boots. "If... if... if you kill it, I'm sure my son will come back to life. It's a charm. That beast has my son's soul in its insides. It has to be freed so it can come back to my embrace." I bent down and offered her my hand so she could stand up. She kissed my jade ring. Caressed my fingers with her cheeks. I could feel the tears running down to my nails. Cold tears like that stone palace. A frozen heart that had come to a halt in that fatal moment.

The table was well decked out. A fire lit up the room, which was lacking in useful objects. Everybody sat in their respective chairs. Upright. Elegant. Clean. Awaiting my presence. They fixed their gazes on me. I felt them like needles pricking my skin. The Count gestured to me to take a seat. Bishop del Riego was at his left. At his right, the Collector, still with that listless expression. Johan was there as well, next to an old blind man who I guessed was his father. Opposite, a plump, taciturn woman. Amaina's single sister. I felt like opening the door and legging it back to Luiçiana.

There were two cockerels. A bowl full of all the parts a pig could contain. Another piled high with roasted chestnuts. Potatoes. Cabbage. Apple pie. Strawberry pie. Wine. I sat at the head of the table. Two women started serving food on every plate. They were silent. Subjected. The room was adorned with oak furniture and the odd painting hanging on the wall. There were no flowers. No smiles in the paintings. There were crosses. Marble virgins. A fire. Lit candles. And solemnity.

"I don't know why, Mr d'Ourantes, I thought you would be older," remarked the Count with a piece of cockerel in his mouth.

"It's not the first time I've heard that," I replied sardonically. "I've lived for a number of years. I don't know if they're many or few – they are what they are."

"I trust Johan helped you on the road to our beautiful Valley."

Johan went red. Looked up from the plate to catch my eye. Didn't dare and looked back down at the plate. His father placed a hand on his shoulder, awaiting a favourable answer on my part. The old man was withered by time. His skin was excessively wrinkled. Scars on a bald head covered in markings. I couldn't see any resemblance between them. The old man was small and short. Johan, despite his exaggerated shyness, like he was the others' servant, was tall and upright. Perhaps Johan had taken entirely after his mother. The eyes. The eyebrows. The curvature of the lips. The greasy hair. At that moment, I realized he wasn't related to Mateu Pelaiz, former collector of Constança Valley.

"Yes. He helped. He was very useful on the journey. He will turn into a great man."

The father smiled and patted his son's shoulder. Then whispered something in his ear. "I'm proud of you." Not exactly those words, but something along those lines to express his satisfaction, I'm sure of that. The bishop had drunk three glasses of wine. He needed them to sate the thirst of that fat, greasy body. He raised his hand and asked one of the serving women to put more chestnuts on his plate. At this juncture, the women started offering chestnuts to everybody seated at the table. I refused.

"Forgive me if I ask you a question," said Bishop del Riego. "I've always wanted to hear stories from the *Americas*. You know how soldiers exaggerate when they come back from war…"

"I'm a soldier," I interrupted him.

"Yes, yes, but not that kind of soldier. You know what I mean. Your family fought for the true faith. They say His Holiness holds you in high esteem."

"Soldiers also die for the faith, sir, and for the *Queen*, and for the *King* before that, for the country, the Church... Right now, at this very moment, they're dying. They die, and die, and die... falling far from their homes. While you are here, by the fire and a table full of food, they carry on dying."

"And I keep them in my prayers, I assure you," the bishop made the sign of the cross. "They fight for what they believe in. Fighting for *God* and the *Queen* is a path to eternal glory."

"In which case, why don't you go and fight?"

Silence. Everybody stared at me. Even old Mateu Pelaiz, and he was blind. No doubt, in the empty darkness he discerns, my words suggested to him an unpleasant figure. That figure was me. The Collector placed a knife on the table. The Count put a piece of bread on his plate. The servants whispered to each other with wide open eyes. The bishop burst out laughing. He had to take a napkin to wipe away the bits of meat that had flown out of his mouth with so much guffawing.

"Oh, dear me... Imagine me at war! No, milord. That would be ridiculous! I wouldn't last a minute. No. *God* puts every man in the place where he belongs. He made me a messenger of his divine word. He makes others bear arms."

Someone entered the hall. It was Amaina de Guimaraes. The Count stood up abruptly and went towards her. Took her by the elbow. She gestured to him to say she was fine. She was wearing a long, black dress that reached down to her feet. Amaina was a tall, slim woman. She had a good figure. Smooth, dark hair that flowed beneath her narrow waist like a crystal-clear waterfall. Her eyes were red, a sign of her recent sorrow over the death of her son. Ricardo de Guimaraes led her by the hand to her chair. She sat down slowly. The servants quickly placed a plate in front of Amaina, but she indicated that she didn't want anything. She hadn't come to eat.

"You must forgive my attitude, Mr d'Ourantes, the loss of my son is very recent, sometimes I can't control myself."

"You have nothing to apologize for, madam."

"I felt very happy when my husband managed to find you. They say you're the best wolf hunter. What is it they call you?" she turned towards the Count. "What was it, my love?"

Ricardo de Guimaraes chewed slowly. Looked up. Swallowed. It was an unpleasant, forced, even bitter swallow.

"I understand Mr d'Ourantes doesn't like that nickname, milady."

Amaina swung around in surprise. Expelled air. All the air such a lean body could contain. I would have said she turned excessively white, but the truth is she was a pale-skinned woman. A ghost. A beautiful ghost.

"Don't you like the nickname? I seem to recall it wasn't bad. No, it wasn't bad, was it, my love?" she glanced back in the Count's direction.

"Three Wolves. That's what they called me. Three Wolves."

Nobody said a word. Ricardo de Guimaraes was right. I didn't like this nickname I had been given in Red Mountain. Those distrustful villagers hired me because half their flock of sheep turned up dead in three days. I had never seen it rain so much as it did in Red Mountain. All the time. It was a drizzling rain. That was why all the villagers looked so sulky. Gritted their teeth. As if they were in this world against their will. On my first night in the village, the wolf attacked again. Seven more sheep. Almost all the wealth of Red Mountain had disappeared in a matter of days. Days of rain beating on the roofs. On the clothes hanging on the line. On the grass of the meadow. Two men from the village came with me. We each carried a torch. They were rooted to the spot when the wolf appeared in front of us. It was a silver wolf. They call it that because its fur is grey and, when it gets wet, it looks as if it's wearing shiny armour. The two men resembled youngsters confronting their childhood demons. Frightening stories on stormy nights. They were paralyzed. The wolf bared its teeth, ready to attack. Threw itself straight at us.

"That's it!" exclaimed Amaina. "You killed three wolves with your bare hands and saved the men who were with you. Isn't that right?"

I raised my eyebrows.

"Something like that..."

The two men, full of fear, ran off through the pines. Disappeared into the mist. I was lying on the wet ground, holding the wolf's snout in my hands, while it tried to open its mouth to get in the first bite. Its breath was warm. It climbed into the air and evaporated. Suddenly, in among the stones and dead oak branches, I glimpsed five wolf pups. The five of them were watching the struggle between two animals. Me on the one side. The silver wolf on the other. I knew then this wasn't a male, but a female. I gazed into its eyes and conveyed the message. It calmed down. Took two steps back. I stood up. Ran my hand over its back. When I reached the village, they all thought I was dead. The two men who'd fled with their tails between their legs had let it be known in the tavern of Red Mountain that we'd been surrounded by three wolves. "As big as crags. Lithe as cats. With sharp teeth and bloodshot eyes." When they saw me come in without so much as a scratch, they clasped their heads. Stared at me like I was a walking miracle. "He killed three wolves! Three wolves!"

"Tell me, sir. How is life in Luiçiana? I'm always asking Ricardo to take me there, but he says it's too dangerous…"

Boooom! The bishop banged his fist on the table. His wine glass fell over, spilling the liquid on the wood. One of the serving women hurried to clear up the mess. The bishop gestured to say now was not the time to start cleaning. The woman went back to her original position. Del Riego tore some meat off the poultry leg he was holding.

"Milady," he spat between his teeth, "what can you expect from people who don't respect the *Queen* or *God*? I don't understand why Her Majesty doesn't send troops so the serenity of the Church can return to those lands."

I wanted to think about my answer. Once again. But once again I couldn't help myself.

"She doesn't send them because she knows she would lose the fight," I interrupted. "For Her Majesty, it's better to ignore Luiçiana than to waste money and men trying to get it back. Luiçiana is a tiny piece of land that has nothing more than rebellious men and a leafy forest. The *Queen* has other, more urgent problems right now. The empire is running out of empire."

Luiçiana is still an itch in the Church's wounds. They got kicked out. The monastery and temples were plundered, the booty shared out among the neighbours. There are priests who continue to lend their spiritual services, but they don't agree with the current status of the Church. They say majesty and wealth are not attributes of *God*. They live a vow of poverty. Eat only what they need. Have no possessions.

"How about Gothard,[1] Mr d'Ourantes? Shouldn't we try to take that back?" intervened the Count suddenly.

I took a chestnut in my hand. Placed it carefully on my tongue. Let it dissolve between my saliva and teeth. Felt the taste filtering through to my tongue. Savoured the moment. Swallowed.

"Take Gothard back? Since when did it form part of the Empire?"

Ricardo de Guimaraes stared at me in surprise.

"I mean, conquer it," he continued. "They have a silver mine that could be very useful to the crown and the *Kingdom*."

There was the supreme reason. Silver. Money.

----

[1] The setting of Abel Tomé's previous novel, also available in English, *Night of the Crow* (Small Stations Press, 2022).

"Have you ever been to Gothard, Lord Count?"

He shook his head.

"It's an impenetrable island. It has steep walls made of hard, rigid rock. Then there's the long bridge, always ready to fall down. It's impossible to attack with ships, the sea is full of currents that sweep the ships onto jagged rocks by the cliffs. And then there are its cannons. Its people know how to fight. How to defend themselves. And they are full of hatred. Full of an indescribable hatred towards us. I was there once. One time they tried to conquer it. I shall remember it to my dying day. It was hell. Thousands died. We never had a chance of winning. Never. We didn't even get close to the coast. We didn't step on dry land. It's an accursed island."

## THE LEAVES UNHOOKED THEMSELVES FROM TREES

"They say, say, say… he talks to tr… tr… tr… trees," they whispered.

"I heard he understands the language of animals."

Santiago and Lois the Stutterer were murmuring. It wasn't necessary to strain my ears because deep down they both wanted me to hear them. The Count suggested they go with me in search of the wolf. Apparently they know the wood better than anyone in the Valley. Santiago was born in the village of Holy Fountain. He was responsible for training the Count's dogs. He took them into mountain thickets and things like that. He didn't look very clever to me. Small. Lean. He looked at you with distrustful eyes. They all look at you like that in this place. Lois the Stutterer had had a very serious case of influenza when he was a child. He spent almost three months in bed. The boy had got lost when his father and brothers were taking the Count's oxen to the palace stables. He was found three days later on Snowy Peak, a rocky, pointed mountain that covers the north face of the Valley.

"Cruaaaaaghhh! Cruaaaaaghhh!" I imitated a crow.

Santiago nudged the Stutterer and gestured with his head towards me.

"See! See! He speaks the language of the crow."

The Stutterer made the sign of the cross. Once. Twice.

"So it was here the wolf was last sighted. Right?" I asked.

"Yes, sir. Here. In *Cliffs' Refuge*. Among those rocks," he pointed. "You're... not like the others..."

"What others?" I asked.

The two of them walked towards me, crunching leaves beneath their feet. Santiago got a little too close, and so I gently pushed him away. The Stutterer stayed behind him, as if he was afraid. It was strange because the Stutterer was a tall, strong man who towered over the shorter Santiago. They were a striking couple.

"The others, sir. The other hunters."

"I'm not the first?"

Santiago turned around and looked at the Stutterer.

"No, sir. There have been three. And they all brought tools. You're not like them."

"What were they like?"

"Different."

Santiago and the Stutterer led me to a den one of the hunters, Gonçaluo Longo, a taciturn man with a slight Portuguese accent, had got them to build. There was a cave in the ground full of brambles. Surrounded by a rickety wall. They went on the hunt with the intention of driving the wolf towards the den. What they found in the ditch wasn't a wolf, but a bear. It was wounded. At the start of the month, it had rained for a whole week. The mountain was wet. Gonçaluo slipped and fell into the hole. The bear didn't pass up this opportunity to take its revenge.

"App... app... apparently you... can talk to... to... the tr... ee... s..."

"Who said that?"

"Tha... that's what... I heard."

"It's a lot of nonsense."

This mountain doesn't want to speak. Just like the wood in Luiçiana. They are resentful and don't say a word. It's an old wood. An old man sitting on a chair anchored to the earth. In the *jungle*, I learnt to enter into communion with nature. I was taught to hear what it says. Animals, trees, the river... Lots of people would say I'm mad, but I'm not. There's something inexplicable between us. A union we are unaware of. *Nexus*. I'm not talking about *God*, something else. There's a common language we do not know. Us, them, the wood, birds, water... we're one and the same. One and the same. It's not like that here. Here, the link has been broken. All the same, I remember what I once was, even though it makes me ashamed. Even though I'm condemned. I don't need the paraphernalia used by other hunters. Hunting a wolf is like hunting a person.

"And the second hunter?"

"The second?" continued Santiago. "The second was from a distant town. I can't remember which. We called him del Castillo. He... hunt... well, it was women really. He took off with Bieito the stonemason's wife. She was a young girl, you know? Bieito has money and reached a deal with the family to marry her when she was only fourteen. Then, along came del Castillo on the back of that white horse... It was Bieito's fault for putting him up in his house. Apparently he paid a bounty hunter to kill him and bring her back."

"Oh my!"

The Stutterer nodded. The wind lifted a bit and started moving the branches. A crow. A squirrel scurrying across the path. It was cold. The afternoon was fading like a fire. The sun had yet to appear. There's no sun here. The sky is a misty outbreath. Grey. Sad.

"Don... don... don't... you want... to know... wh... who the thi... thi... third wolf hu... hunter was?"

"Truth is I couldn't care less."

I turned around and walked into the wood, whose thickness closes off the paths made by men.

"It... it was... him... wh... who... saw... the... the... wo... lf."

I stopped. "It was him who saw the wolf." Interesting. I obviously had to ask.

"Who was it?"

The two of them looked at each other.

"A foreigner, milord. He turned up here after the death of the Count's son. Offered to capture it. Seems he'd been pursuing the wolf for quite some time. He called it the *creature*. He cornered it, but didn't manage to hunt it down. The next day, he disappeared. Rumour has it he's in Snowy Peak, in the House of the Viços."

"How do I get there?"

Santiago came over and grabbed me by the shirt. The Stutterer took two steps backwards. "N... n... n... n... no."

"No. You can't go to Snowy Peak. In the House of the Viços, there are only dangerous people. You understand. Thieves, murderers... worse than that. Children of the devil.

"What's the foreigner's name?"

Santiago fixed me with his eyes and shook his head. From behind, the Stutterer lifted his chin and raised his hand.

"Ví... Ví... Víctor, sir."

# I SHALL NOT FEAR MISTAKE

To reach Snowy Peak, you have to take a narrow path that climbs little by little, bend after bend. In the Valley, it's called the *Cat's Tail*. More often than not, it's covered in mud. Near the summit, the wind is icy and biting, like an invisible knife. Snow accumulates on the path, and sometimes it's impossible to pass. Santiago and the Stutterer pleaded with me not to go. I insisted that the House of the Viços would not be worse than war or the *jungle*. They didn't know the devastating significance of those two words because they'd never left the Valley. The Count didn't like me going. I told him it was necessary to talk to this Víctor in order to hunt the wolf. If he was the only one who'd met it face to face, then he could describe the animal to me. I need to have a picture of the wolf. To draw it with my mind. To be transformed. To see with its eyes. To step with its paws. To smell with its snout. If the wood doesn't speak, then I need to be the wolf.


The views from the *Cat's Tail* are beautiful. You can make out the thickness of the Valley. Strokes of green that come together in a spiral. From here, it looks like a peaceful, pleasant place. A sanctuary in this warlike, hate-filled world.

As I climb towards the summit, the wind gets stronger. The horse finds it difficult to go on. It's cold, and the snow is starting to be a problem. Near the House of the Viços is a wooden sign stuck to a post by the side of the road. On it, an engraving: "You are about to set foot in Snowy Peak. There is no King. No Church. No law." What with the wind and the snow beating against my face, I could barely make out the lamps of the House of the Viços. In such conditions, it struck me as strange that they should be lit. I unhooked one of them and led the horse to the stables. Counted seven horses in there. Went back outside. Put the lamp back in its place. Glanced at the Valley, but saw only a white perspective.

There is a door. It seems closed to the world, as if another universe existed inside. It's a wooden door. Thick, apparently. It has a golden knocker in the shape of a fox's head. I banged on it. A small hatch opened above the knocker. All I could see were some thick, chapped lips immersed in a black beard.

"Who is it?" barked a deep voice.

"Someone who wants to come in to shake off the cold accompanying him."

Intentional silence. The wind whistled, as if demanding attention. A crow cawed in the distance, and the sound echoed in the depths of the void.

"Are you afraid of death?"

"No."

"Why not?"

"Because I've faced it a hundred times."

Another silence.

"Where?"

"In places I do not wish to remember. In places I do not wish to go back to."

The lips smiled.

"Coming in doesn't mean you'll go out."

Now I was the one who smiled.

"Who said I wanted to go out? Open the door."

"Or else..."

"Or else I'll burn this fucking house down with all of you in it."

The third silence was the longest. An abyss on the other side of a cliff. Death down at the bottom. The impact is some time coming. Under my feet, the wood splintered. I felt the earth trembling. As if Snowy Peak was tired of seeing everything from on high and wished to contemplate the world at the right height. The same crow as before perched on one of the wooden beams. Cruaaaaaaghhhhh. It jumped off the beam and ducked towards me with outspread wings. I brushed it aside. The door opened.

"This is the House of the Viços. There is no *King*. There is no Church. There is no law. You are free to come in. As for going out..."

I nodded, as if grateful that the door had been opened. Inside, everything was different. Another world confined within four walls. A room of red, scarlet wood. Stag antlers adorned the walls. Mirrors of different sizes. A painting of some ancestor of the Viços. They gave me hostile looks. Through gritted teeth. Frowning. Threatening. And, in a fraction of a moment, time stopped. Everything was a picture. A scene with movement contained in the painting. In the mix of colours. Time started turning again, impelled by its own inertia. Two men chatted around a table. They were armed. Another four played cards. Shouted at each other. Jabbed their fingers. Issued threats. Another man leant on a corner of the bar, staring at me. He had a black, trimmed beard. On his waist, he carried a sickle.

"A wine."
"We don't have wine here. Only pulque."
The man with the sickle lifted his head and stared at me. He had marks on his forehead. Like lots of savages in the *jungle* who wore lines and drawings on their skin. He leant on the bar again, as if to continue a sleep he had left unfinished. The barman served me a jug of pulque. He was a chubby guy with a scarf covering his head. I pulled out a coin and placed it on the counter. He took it and waved it in front of my nose.

"No! We don't accept the *Queen's* coins here! There is no *Queen* here! This isn't worth shit here. This is the House of the Viços! And I am Viço number seven. Gold, silver, or something of interest. If you have nothing else to offer, you can get the hell out of here before I kill you!"

Time stopped once again. Everybody fixed their eyes on me, once again. I stood there, feeling indifferent. And saw how a scarlet-leaved flower behind the counter twisted and turned and grew a whole span. I rubbed my eyes. Thought it must have been an illusion. But I could swear it wasn't. I could swear it was real.

"I have nothing of value except for a few of these coins," I gestured towards the coin he was holding.

"A curse on the *Queen!*" Viço number seven chucked the coin at the front door. He wiped the saliva that had gathered at the corners of his lips on his shirt sleeves. And took a swig from the jug of pulque he had served me. Pointed at my knife. "And that? Now that could be useful... I like it."

I sighed. Looked around. Time remained stationary. Every one of those wretches had a hand on his weapon. Even the sleepy guy next to me, his head resting on the bar, was gripping the handle of his sickle.

"This knife will leave here with me. It's more valuable than my own life."

"Well then, you're making it easy for me. The knife will remain here, and you will leave the House of the Viços on your back."

"I'm sorry to disappoint you, but that's not how it's going to be."

A whistle rang out from one end of the room. Fuuuuuuuuuuuuuuuuuuuuuiiiiiiiiiii! There was the figure of a person cloaked in darkness. A mysterious figure who was alone.

"On me!" he said.

He tossed a coin from far away which happened to land right in front of me. The coin span on its axis on top of the counter. A chance event, but a surprising one. It was made of gold.

"There's your payment," continued the voice of that man with a heavy foreign accent. "Nobody's going to die today."

Time started moving slowly. Everyone went back to what they were doing before that tense conversation. Viço number seven nodded, as if accepting what the stranger had said. Served me my pulque. Without reply. The figure raised a hand, inviting me to go and sit with him in that dark space. The shadow, once again.

# NIGHT WILL NEVER BE

"Víctor, I presume."

"Exactly, *mein Freund*."

"Víctor…"

"Víctor Frankens… Just call me Víctor," he smiled. "You won't be able to pronounce my surname. You don't have Germanic languages."

"You speak our language well."

"I speak lots of languages. German, English, Italian, French… It took you longer than I expected, *Herr* d'Ourantes."

"Were you expecting me?"

"Most anxiously."

Despite his weary appearance, Víctor F. had the refined air of someone who came from a well-positioned family. He was a little scruffy, but there was an elegance about his clothing, as if everything occupied its rightful place. In front of him was a jug of beer. He grabbed it. *Prost.* Banged it against mine and took a swig.

"I had to show them how to make beer," he said, pointing at Viço number seven. "I can't bear that stuff they served you."

"It seems you softened the Viços."

"Baaaaaahhhh... No, *mein Freund*, don't forget above the *Queen*, the Church, and the law is this," Víctor F. took a bag full of gold coins out of his pocket. "Gold!"

He wiped the foam off his lips. Raised a hand and indicated "two" with his fingers. Viço number seven nodded. The wind lashed against the windowpanes. Inside, everything was red. Outside, white. A curious mix of colours. Blood spattered on snow.

"Over to you then."

Víctor raised his eyebrows in surprise.

"Whatever for, *Herr* d'Ourantes?"

He let out a timid smile.

"If you were expecting me, then I imagine you know why I came."

Viço number seven filled both jugs and bowed his head as a sign of gratitude. He then turned around and walked back to the counter. He walked in a strange way. As if one of his legs wasn't flesh and blood.

"Ahhhhhh... Of course. The wolf. Wolf. Wolf. Wolf," he lifted both hands towards the ceiling.

"The wolf. That's right. What was it like?"

He displayed another smile. More generous, this time.

"No, no, no... *Herr* d'Ourantes," he took a swig of beer. "Before the wolf, we're going to talk about other things. You and me. What do you think?"

I didn't like this attitude on the part of the stranger. I took out my knife and placed it on the table. Rolled up my sleeves. Grabbed hold of the jug.

"You won't need that," he gestured towards the knife with his chin. "Believe me."

"I don't know what the hell you want from me, but I don't have time to mess around. The wolf..."

"Yes, right, the wolf," he interrupted me. "You know something? I didn't come to the Valley in search of some wolf. I was following in the footsteps of a demonic being. When I heard about the death of the Count's son, I deduced the *Dämon* was near. Elizabeth, William..."

Víctor F. stared at a fixed point on the table. As if right then he had laid down his body and his soul had travelled to another place. In the direction of memory. It happens to me all the time. At every moment. The *jungle* is deeply embedded. Mixed with my blood. Coursing down my veins. In every vertex of my body. Víctor came to.

"I knew long before, *Herr* d'Ourantes."

"Knew what?"

"You!" he raised a hand and pointed at me.

"Well now! And how's that?" I leant forwards and propped my elbows on the table. "If you don't mind me asking..."

Víctor gulped another swig of beer without taking his eyes off me. Took out a shiny watch combining gold and silver in carefully engraved lines that formed symbols I didn't recognize. Intersecting lines. Circles. He lifted the lid. Tick! Glanced at the time. Put the watch away without worrying whether those present might try to snatch it from him. To steal. Murder. Although everybody went about their business, in the House of the Viços I had the impression there was a connection. Invisible threads linking people. A union added to a tension that was about to explode. Boom! And yet the stranger wasn't afraid. Víctor paid no attention to the surrounding scene. For him, it was only the two of us in that square of red wood.

"In Ingolstadt," he continued, "there's a secret brotherhood called Roter Mond. Whenever we got together, each member would wear clothes that represented a wild animal. A nocturnal animal. I was the Wolf. Some coincidence, don't you think?" he laughed. "In the brotherhood, we would carry out slightly unethical experiments. You know. Go off to the cemetery and dig up newly buried corpses. Examine them. Take out their organs. Heart. Liver. Kidneys. Brain. Then we'd try to get them to work on their own. Imagine a heart beating without a body! Boom, boomboom, boom, boomboom," Víctor banged the table, imitating the rhythm. "Amazing. The human body is very interesting on the inside. Most people find it disgusting. For me, it was of indescribable beauty. We also investigated unconventional phenomena. Magic. In Ingolstadt library, there's a section called '*Schwarze Bücher*'. The name is carved into the wooden arch," he drew an imaginary arch in the air. "The books are kept in a red cupboard. Now that I think about it, just as red as this place," he lifted his eyes and glanced around. "The doors are locked. Even so, we managed to open the door of the cupboard. Every Thursday, we would go in search of a book. They were very old. Some written in languages we didn't know. They talked about the devil. Possessed children. Rituals. One night, we took a damp, ancient manuscript with anecdotes of soldiers who'd fought against American tribes in the *jungle*. Most witnesses described naked men with painted, perforated bodies. Dances by the light of the moon. Poisonous arrows. Cannibalism. But there was one account that really surprised us, *Herr* d'Ourantes. The story came from the voice of a certain Alessio da Montorfano, a Franciscan monk who looked after the sick arriving at Treva Monastery in Italy. Defeated people with no reason to stay in the world would go there. Most were men who had been traumatized by war. By situations they had experienced first-hand. Horrifying images etched in here," he pointed to his head. "They wanted to die. Monk Alessio keeps notes of the conversations he has with them. There are some interesting things. Sorrow, sadness, are highly destructive, and the stories that lead to them can be very tragic. But, among all those notes, there was one chapter that occupied a good number of pages called '*La volontà*'. It contains the testimony of a member of *La volontà*, a group of bloody mercenaries hired on the orders of Pope Clement VII. Their mission was to enter the Amazon *jungle* and take Christianity to the Vermelhos, a tribe located in the furthest reaches of that green corner of the New World. A Portuguese expedition had come across this tribe unexpectedly. Only one soldier had survived. He related how the Vermelhos didn't have weapons. How the trees, water, animals... attacked the soldiers as if the natives controlled them. You understand? But he also said the tribe had lots of gold. Tools, figures, adornments... all made of gold. *La volontà* was formed of twelve men. Each was assigned the name of one of the twelve apostles so nobody would know the others' names and where they came from. The twelve mercenaries were well known for their atrocities in battle. Savage, pitiless warriors. They were commanded by a soldier who was referred to as *Peter*. He was the worst of the lot, and also the only one entrusted with the real aim of that mission, which was to seize the Vermelhos' gold. They decided not to carry firearms. Only knives, bows, and arrows. The road was hard. Like everything in the *jungle*. The twelve reached the tribe. Gazed through the vegetation at the huts in trees adorned with gold figures. The natives with their red skin going about their business. Children scampering between their mothers' legs. Women with plaited hair bringing water from the river. They spent seven days in hiding, watching the tribe. The men were small, albeit well defined, and all had long hair. As the Portuguese soldier had said, they didn't carry weapons. They had a chief. Zoriah. A medium-sized man with a gold bracelet that went all the way up his arm to his shoulder. Zoriah had a son. Tarthai. And a daughter. Lizah. When the seven days were up, *Peter* decided to enter the village. The sun was sinking behind the *jungle*. Their intention was simple. To assassinate Zoriah while he was having dinner on the *throne*, a chair formed by the roots of a tree that was swallowed up by its own height. To assassinate him in front of all the Vermelhos. It was well known that, for many tribes, killing the chief, the spiritual leader, meant subjecting the other savages. *Peter* shot an arrow straight at the chief's heart. He missed. It went through Zoriah's shoulder, but he didn't even flinch. Nobody said a word. *Peter* raised his sword and shouted. *La volontà* attacked the tribe. The Vermelhos stood there, staring at these outsiders shouting and racing towards them with merciless intent. Then the ground trembled. The trees twisted and turned. The twelve came to a halt in the village clearing and glanced around. The *jungle* was rebelling against the invaders."

## YOU STING AGAIN!

Time is dense. I can shape it with my hands. It takes the form of strange men gazing at our table. As if they'd been listening at every moment. Waiting for the right time to pile on top of us. Once again. How many is that? I don't like this place. I'm in a dream. A nightmare. But it's not a dream. Or a nightmare. What is it? The House of the Viços. Someone knocked at the door. Someone went over to it. Asked the necessary questions. I don't know if they were the same I was asked. I'm not even sure it was the same man. This one was slim and clean. Mine had a deep, gravelly voice, like a shout from a cliff. I glimpsed his thick, unkempt beard through the grille. This one was clean shaven. He opened the door. In came a dwarf. A *half man* carrying an adult roe deer. He dumped it on the table. Said something to Viço number seven. Nodded. Everybody else exclaimed in delight. Except for us. Everything went back to its rhythm.

"Are you going to tell me about the wolf of Constança? I'm fed up of listening to your nonsense."

Víctor muttered something in his language. Glanced at the ceiling. Then in front.

"I already told you, *Herr* d'Ourantes. First, my story."

"What does that have to do with me? I'm not interested in your story."

"Not long to go now. Believe me."

I stared at him with indifference. Indifference. Turn around. Reject the world. Be conscious only of your own existence. The only existence you can be aware of. The only existence worth the effort. The rest is shadows that live alongside your existence. Smoky images. You can pass right through them. Dissipate them with a puff of breath. Legs fleeing from somebody who's trying to trap you. Hands grasping the sickle that cuts grass like heads off a body. Lips that kiss. Teeth that bite until they make you bleed. Water running through the rocks of a stream. Mother washing clothes while singing happily. Father will hit her when he gets home, and everything will go black. The fox in the snow isn't shivering with cold. The shout of a boy frightened by his sister. Flames devouring the village. The touch of a sword piercing skin. A soldier raping a native.

"*Herr* d'Ourantes, *Herr*..."

Víctor clicked his fingers in front of my nose. His eyes were wide open. I came to. Another of those moments when I let myself fall while being awake.

"Forgive me... Sometimes I seem to be here, but really I'm not," I said.

"Right. I know what that is. Ever since that accursed night. That *devil* that took away everything. *Vater*!"

The stranger's presence made me feel uneasy. Not afraid. I'm not afraid. But he put me on edge. Gave me a bitter taste in my mouth. With that mournful, mysterious face of his. I didn't know what he was talking about. Sentences with questions. He had a turbulent, black past. A past that changed him completely. I bet he came from a well-to-do family. One of those young gentlemen who go to study abroad. Now he was a rebel. A man on his last legs in search of someone he called the *devil*. That *devil* seemed to have killed somebody who was important for him. Until he found him, he wasn't going to get rid of that sorrow.

"Listen," I said. "We've been here too long. The Count wasn't too keen on my coming up the mountain. I don't care what you think, but I need to know what the wolf was like."

"You know what happened to those soldiers, *Herr* d'Ourantes?"

I let out a lament in the form of a sigh that vanished into the air. Warm, reddish air. Needless to say. I gestured angrily with my hand so the stranger would continue. He smiled. I wanted to strangle him with my bare hands, see his eyes on the verge of exploding because of a lack of air. I restrained myself.

"The roots of the trees pushed to the surface. They attacked the twelve from *La volontà*. Can you imagine? Pitiless soldiers waving swords at the roots of trees moving like snakes. In amidst the chaos of battle. You know. Shouts, blood, sweat... clinging to this world with everything you've got. *Peter* hadn't forgotten his strategy, so in that battle that was almost lost he shot another arrow to kill Zoriah. Again, he missed his target. Tarthai got in the way, and the arrow drove deep into his heart. Zoriah watched as his son hurtled forwards and fell into his arms. He let out a shout that was heard in every vertex of the *jungle*. When *Peter* turned to see what was happening with the battle, all the members of *La volontà* were in pieces on the damp ground. He was the only survivor. The only one still standing, still alive. Zoriah ordered his arrest."

# AND ON THE STRANGEST SEA

"Wolf. Big. Thick, white fur."

"White?"

"Yes. White as snow. Beautiful. Nature is curious, you know? So is *God*. But in this case *He* had nothing to do with it. I'd never seen a white wolf. It struck me as an animal to worship, not to fear," he stared thoughtfully at the table.

"Didn't you attack it?"

"No," he raised his head. "It had cornered me between these rocks. It bared its teeth. Grrrrrrrrrrrrrrrr," he imitated the sound. "I was ready. I had my knife in my hand so I could stick it in the wolf's throat if it threw itself at me. But it didn't. It looked at me. A man on one side. A wolf on the other. It had these crystal-clear, gleaming eyes. It licked its snout and disappeared. *Auf Wiedersehen!*"

I went down the mountain. Along the way, I turned over what the *stranger* had told me. In the end, I didn't let him finish his story. I couldn't waste any more time sitting there, listening to his ghosts. He got mad. I got even madder. And the two men who were chatting came over. One was wearing a hat and had a twisted, scarred nose. The other was tall and thin, missing a piece of his left ear, the result of a bite. The man in the hat asked Víctor for his watch. Threatened to kill him.

"The watch," he said in a deep voice.

"What watch?" replied Víctor mockingly.

"The one in your pocket," he gestured with his head. "The one that shines so much."

The man with the gnawed ear came up beside me. Wiped his lips on his sleeves. Pulled up his trousers. Greeted me with a hostile grunt. "Brrrrrrrrrrr." Glanced at my knife, which was lying motionless on the table. Put out a hand to take it. I smashed the glass of beer on his hand so hard that one of his fingers came flying off. He shouted. Bled. Held his hand and stared with distorted features at his amputated finger. The man in the hat turned around. Víctor grabbed my knife and stuck it in his neck. He fell on the floor of the House of the Viços. The man with the ear saw how a thick, slow pool of blood was coming out of his companion, wetting the new corpse's clothing. He opened the door and fled. Nobody said anything. They were like stone statues. Viço number seven came out from behind the bar and grabbed the dead man by the feet.

Dragged him towards the end of the corridor. The dwarf who had brought a roe deer stared at the trail of blood. A red line. Then turned around and gestured towards Víctor in greeting. The *stranger* responded by lifting his head. Everything went back to a kind of normality that was far from being normal.

I took my leave of Víctor. Not a particularly warm farewell. Even so, despite our tense encounter, I felt a certain connection between the two of us. I know what a man's metamorphosis is like. Sorrow, pain, wrath, anger... a heap of contradictory emotions that change your personality. And you're no longer the same. You're somebody else. That was why I didn't give Víctor's attitude too much importance. I understood it. He was searching for a *devil*. And the *devil* would finish him off. Sometimes you can see a man's future through his eyes. In the mixed lines and colours. You have to look hard. He was going to die in a place as cold as this one. Just as far away. Sea all around. Ice. Just before letting out his last breath, he would realize the search for vengeance had served no purpose. It had distanced him from the world. Reality. Turned him into a base man. A solitary. A stone. And nothing had brought back the loved ones he'd lost along the way. Víctor F. would realize, deep down, the *devil* was himself.

Outside, the wind whistles as if calling to someone. I hope it's not me. I'm not used to the cold. The *jungle* isn't cold. Not cold in that sense. It's cold in other ways. The cold I carry inside. Ever since I left. That cold. That one.

The road is covered in snow. Always snow. It's called Snowy Peak for a reason. Places have logical names. Provoked by some justified cause. The horse finds it difficult to walk. The wind beats hard. Against my chest. My arms. My legs. Against everything that gets in the way. Everything that obstructs its invisible, but merciless progression.

The road down from Snowy Peak is not the same as the way up. You descend on the other side of the mountain. It's just as hard and leads to Valley Arch, one of many ways into Constança Valley wood. About halfway, the mist dissipates, and the green hues of the trees at this time of year become visible. Further down, the snow disappears, revealing mud and stones. A stream descends next to the road. People in the Valley call it "the fountain of tears" and say the water has healing properties, but it's just snowmelt.

Valley Arch is an enormous arch formed by the crowns of two interlinking oaks. The end result is a half moon that acts as a natural entrance to the wood.

The wood is warmer than the mountain. Rays enter through an opening in a rebellious cloud and intermingle on the leaves. Yellow. Green. It's the first time I've seen sunlight since I got here. Perhaps it's a sign that everything's over and I can go in peace. Let the body disintegrate beneath the earth. Let nature do its job.

The horse needs a rest. Time to catch its breath and think about its horsy things. I let it. It's earned a rest. It lies in a clearing, making the most of the sudden warmth. I lie next to it and place my head on its stomach. Its breathing is agitated and tired. I close my eyes. Enjoy the moment. Savour the sun, which tastes of bitter orange. Pass my hand over the grass. The earth's hair. Think this would be a good place to die. A good moment to die. But it's not going to be like that. "Until you feel the same sorrow, until you feel the same pain." I remember his words.

## NO BLOSSOM STAYED AWAY

"Make the most of it. This won't last long. Constança Valley is grey. Always. All year round."

I turned. I had one man aiming at me. And three more standing there. They all had a blue line going from one ear to the other, passing through their eyes. They reminded me of a tribe from the *jungle*.

"What the hell? Who are you?"

A woman came out of the thickness of the wood. She also had a blue line. She wore a white dress that reached down to her knees. On her hair, a crown of flowers. She put a hand on the shoulder of the man aiming at me. Lowered his arm.

"Calm down, sir. We're not going to harm you."

"Then I won't harm you, either."

The woman smiled. She had orange, glistening hair. She was barefoot.

"You've come from Snowy Peak, haven't you?"

"Have you been watching me?"

She smiled again. Came over and grabbed my hand. I let her.

"No. We're not watching you. But you're in Valley Arch. So I suppose you've come from the mountain."

She turned my hand over. Started touching the lines on my palm. Following the wrinkles. Lines. Nodded. Whispered indecipherable words. In another language. An old, ancient language. It sent a shiver down my spine. I pulled my hand away.

"What are you then, a witch?"

She fixed her eyes on me so deeply that for the tiniest of moments I was in her body. And I heard the wood talking. All energy filters through my soul. The same energy as the *jungle*. Strong. Warm. I was the wood. I felt like crying. There was pain. Suffering. Death. But there was also an air of indescribable beauty. It was a spark. Contained hope. A barely discernible spot. The witch fell to the ground. I was in her body. She, in mine. She saw horrifying things. From the ground, she looked up. Adopted a startled expression.

"I'm not a witch," she said. "I'm an *Eadar*."

"A what?"

"An *Eadar*, an interpreter of the wood," she stood up. "We are Breços. The community that espouses the old religion. The one of our ancestors. We fight against the imposition of Bishop del Riego. A cruel, bloody murderer."

"I heard about you. I also saw what they do to you. Three hanging at the Gates of Holy Victory. A father. A mother. A child. Swinging in the mist. And crows pecking their entrails."

One of the men with her started weeping. She went over and stroked his back. Said a few words to him. Kissed him on the cheek.

"That was Breixo's sister's family," she turned and gestured towards him. "The bishop had them hung from the gates of Constança village. They lived in a hut in the wood. The Collector and his men came at night. Destroyed everything. They're like beasts. They always act like that. They burnt the hut. Took them prisoner. The child was eight. They didn't care. They imprisoned them in the cells of the palace. The next day, they hung them on the bishop's orders. Without a trial. For being pagan and for going against the true faith. The true faith. What nonsense. They weren't the first. We have to stop them dead. We will stop them."

"So what are you going to do?"

"Tell me, what does one do in such cases?"

The *Eadar* walked slowly backwards. The crowns of the trees swayed gently. The birds sung amidst the leaves and the yellow colours of the rays. Serenity. She stood next to her companions. Took off the crown of flowers and tossed it to the ground. Stepped on it with her bare feet. The flowers dried instantly. The sun stopped filtering through the trees. Everything became grey. Storm.

"You know why you can't hear it?" she continued.

I didn't know what she was talking about.

"What?" I asked incredulously.

"This. All of this," she raised her arms and gestured around with her body. "You also, in a way, are an *Eadar*. You interpret the wood. But you can't hear the forest of these lands. Right? It seems to be dead. Not to exist. All you perceive is acidic tones and empty words. Silence."

She knew. She was inside me and knew. She saw everything. Everything. Like a spiral. Images. Emotions. Feelings. Everything in an insignificant portion of time. Everything contained. Smashed. It spread in her mind. I felt defeated. I wanted to cry. The tears didn't appear.

"It's true. I can't interpret this wood. It doesn't talk. It just murmurs. Sometimes it's like an insect. Others, like a snake. And from time to time it lets out a horrifying scream. A mother's shout that makes your hair stand on end."

The *Eadar* bent down and picked up the crown of dry flowers. Put it back on her head. The flowers blossomed. Regained their colour and freshness. They were white. They shone on her head as if she was wearing a silver crown. She put a hand on my shoulder.

"You don't hear it because you're not here. You," she prodded my chest with her finger, "are not here. Your body, yes. Flesh, bones, legs, arms... they step on this earth, but that's not important. That doesn't count. What counts is what we carry inside. The outside is false. A mask. Armour. You're not here. You're still there. In that place that wears away at you. Contradictory. You're in the *jungle*."

Ding, dong, ding, dong, ding, dong, ding, dong...
The accelerated sound of the church bell in Constança
dispersed that confusion. Although far away, it stood out
in the thickness of the wood.

"Someone's died. The wolf has attacked again."

# I ROBBED THE WOODS

"I hope going up to Snowy Peak was worth the effort."

"I think so," I replied a little ironically. The Count gave me a smothered look.

"You have to trap that devilish beast before there's another tragedy. The old man was more in the other world than this one, but even so he didn't deserve that death."

"Where's the boy?" I asked.

"Mourning his father."

Mateu Pelaiz had been watering the roses that climb one of the palace's outer walls. He always did that. A little water at first light. And again at dusk. Sometimes he took a bowl of milk and rubbed it on the petals with a cloth. They shine. Glisten. Johan says he did this in order to do something. To be occupied. Men hanging by a thread in their old age do things like that to justify not dying. As a way of telling *God* they're still useful. At that moment, he was alone. Despite being blind and weak, the man moved about the palace corridors very well. He had them in his mind like sheets drawn with a pencil. A map. He didn't find it difficult to reach anywhere. He would walk slowly, with a stick. One leg was damaged – he had to drag it along. The wolf appeared, and Mateu could only wait for it to bite him. One of the villagers found his head in the belly of the forest. The old man's decapitated body collapsed on the roses, which carried on glistening as they were tinged with his blood. This image struck many people as terrible. But not me.

"Are you OK, boy?"

Johan's eyes were moist and full of rage. He wiped away the snot with the sleeve of his shirt. He wanted to suppress his tears, but couldn't.

"How do you think I am? That beast killed my father in the cruellest way possible. He didn't deserve a death like that."

"Nobody deserves a death like that," I didn't believe that. Lots of people do. *I* do.

The boy was sitting on a wooden bench in the palace chapel. A chapel over which presided an image of the Virgin Mary immersed in candles lit by wishes that would be fulfilled in the imagination of the faithful. But never in reality. The Virgin stretched out her arms, as if offering to embrace all those who entered the chapel. She held a rosary. Black beads. Wore a sad expression. They all do. On the wooden base could be read "Our Lady of the Disconsolate in the Valley".

Johan raised his head. Looked at me.

"Why did you go to Snowy Peak? Had you been here, this wouldn't have happened. My... my... my father would still be alive. He would. He would."

"I don't know about that, Johan. Hunting a wolf is not so easy."

"But you're the best at it. They... They say you have powers... You can talk to animals and stuff like that."

I suppressed a guffaw behind my teeth.

"Who are *they*?"

"They. You know. People."

"People come out with all kinds of rubbish, boy. And one who believes the rubbish is as dumb as the one who says it."

Johan lowered his head like an ashamed child. He stayed there, on the bench in the chapel, praying to *God*. The Virgin, pure and radiant, carried on offering an embrace to console those who make do with little. There's a silence in these places that makes your body tremble. The only sound is the sputtering of candles. Fire that doesn't go out and illuminates a room full of crosses and the odd saint badly sculpted in wood. Fire.

The palace corridors are a maze. It's big. Far too big. Aurora lit the way with a candle. She didn't say anything. We reached the room, and she pointed at the door without lifting her eyes from the floor. She wouldn't look at me. I put my hand on the handle and pushed. The room was big, and there was what looked like a comfortable bed. Aurora closed the door very slowly and left without saying anything. Not a word. She obeys and doesn't leave the chapel or church. She's always there, on her knees, her mouth closed. I later found out it seems she doesn't speak to anybody. Coralia, the Count's cook, told me when she was little she played with Aurora and other village children in front of the high cross. "She was a normal child who jumped like a normal girl, laughed like a normal girl, and spoke like a normal girl." Coralia talked nineteen to the dozen while cutting potatoes and onions without shedding a tear. "Everybody knows, sir. It was very tragic. Apparently it was two fugitives who'd escaped from the prison at Suebian Frontier. Aurora was collecting branches the trees had lost after a storm. She was alone. She was a child. And they were bad men." Bad men. Coralia's words resounded in the senses like a shout in the *jungle's* entrails. The *jungle*. Always. In the *jungle*, we were bad men. We destroyed everything. A fire after which nothing would grow. Burnt land.

The bed was wide. Comfortable. The sheets were clean. The following day was going to be hard. The wolf ever present in my thoughts. After the wolf, the memory of White Cliffs. The Count had insisted Lois the Stutterer and Santiago of Holy Fountain accompany me again on my journey through the wood. "Believe me, they know the Valley well, they'll be able to guide you." To start with, I refused, but I ended up giving way before his insistence. I wasn't going to pay much attention to these two clowns. You have to listen to the wood. Its language.

The way the *Eadar* did. She said I wasn't here. My mind and all that. My soul. She said I was in the *jungle*, despite having set foot in the Valley. It was true.

The night in Constança is as silent as Constança itself. It's not like that in Luiçiana. Animals come out of their lairs. Creatures as well. The ones few people see. You can hear a murmur among the trunks of the trees. An unknown language. They stop in front of the door. Scratch the stones of the house. And then scurry away. As if they had lots of feet.

I was woken by a cold touch between the sheets.

"Shhhhhhhhh... Rest easy, milord."

It was the sweet voice of Amaina de Guimaraes, the Count's wife. She was completely naked. She started caressing me very gently. Her skin smelled of mallows and roses. Of mint as well.

"Wh... what are you doing here? I... I don't want any problems," I whispered anxiously.

She closed my lips with a finger. Then kissed me on the neck. Over and over. Again and again and again. I was paralyzed, as if under a spell. Paralyzed by some animal's poison. She carried on kissing me. I began to discover the fine lines of her body. Fingertips going up and down. Soft skin. Sea foam.

"Shhhhhhhhhhh... Rest easy. I'm here to give you pleasure. It's necessary. *He* spoke to me. Told me to come."

She climbed on top of me.

"Who?"

"*God.*"

# IF YOUR SOUL SEESAW

When I woke up, she was no longer there. There was only the space that had previously been occupied by a naked body with long, red hair on white sheets. A living corpse. A body next to mine. Warmth. Touch. Contact. I had kept that sensation deep inside. The sensation that turns your stomach, but isn't disgusting. Quite the opposite. Some call it love. They're wrong. I don't mean that. My love stayed behind in the *jungle*. My love was my sentence. How could he? That was our child. Ours.

Coralia was getting breakfast ready for her lord. She called him *master*. Like she was a dog chained by the neck to a wooden block.

"*Master* will be up in a moment. He told me to give you your breakfast in the hall. You need to be well fed this early in the morning."

"No. I'll have something here. Anything. I don't want a full stomach before tracking a wolf. You never know what you might find."

"But that's what *master* told me. I have to obey *master*, you know," insisted Coralia.

The kitchen table was full of things. The serving women get up very early to prepare their lord and lady's breakfast. Bread, eggs, cake, milk, butter, cheese, apples, chestnuts... Helping Coralia was a tiny girl. She must have been twelve or thirteen. She was dressed in old, tattered clothes. She had just arrived at the palace. She was from a little village up in the mountains. The only daughter of aged parents who could barely work the Count's lands. Three people. Father. Mother. And daughter. Too many mouths to feed.

I cut a slice of bread and offered it to the girl. She was pale, her cheeks very red. She looked at me. Wondered whether to take the bread. Then shook her head.

"What are you doing!" shouted Coralia. "That's for *master*. We can't take it. We eat later. It's forbidden."

I glanced up and down at the cook. She was a chubby woman with enormous breasts. She had also started working in the palace kitchen at an early age. She'd fallen in love with the son of the foreman, an old man they called the Shepherd, who looked after the Count's livestock. When he died, his son inherited his father's position and married Coralia. He was always sidling up to her. She would laugh and tell him to stop. They'd been caught more than once on top of the kitchen table with everything scattered on the floor. Breath. Impulse.

"What was that?"

"The... the... the... Bo... Bo... Bo... Bo..."

"The Boulders, sir," Santiago finished his sentence.

"Why are we going there?"

"Old Pelaiz's head was found nearby. It's a good refuge for a wolf. We need to be careful."

It started raining. Grey sky. Like always. Damp ground. Green, resentful trees. The Stutterer was finding it difficult to keep up. Santiago and I were a step ahead. He tried to catch up with us. He was afraid. Afraid of the wolf. Afraid of everything.

"I heard Lois' story. Did you know him before he got lost in the wood?" I turned my head, gesturing towards him.

Santiago sighed. Walked quickly. Looked ahead. Seeking an objective.

"Don't believe what you hear, sir. There are lots of stories about Lois. But we all know only one of them is true."

"So what really happened?"

Santiago was hunched over, as if counting every step he took. He was always serious. With raised eyebrows and a straight face. He didn't talk much. The bare minimum.

"He was born into the wrong family, sir. Life in the Valley is not easy," he took a deep breath. "Life itself is not easy. His father was a very bad man. He beat him when he was little. Beat all his siblings. Lois would wet himself every time his father walked in. One day, his two older brothers came home after a whole afternoon spent digging the Count's lands. Lois would go with them to lend a hand. When they opened the door, they saw their mother lying on the floor with a bloody face. Their father towering over her. One of the brothers took Lois outside and locked the door. Told him to wait there. Then what had to happen happened. Logical. They killed their father. Stuck a sickle in his neck. Everybody knows, but nobody cared, because the old man deserved it. Home things stay at home."

I turned around again. Lois the Stutterer had fallen behind. I could imagine the childhood of this man with the mind of a child. A childhood in the form of a scar that never heals. And bleeds. Bleeds. Wounded forever. Parents can be pretty hard. Dishing out blows. Children inherit the same attitude. I gestured to Santiago to stop. "Let's wait for Lois," I said. The Stutterer was out of breath. He reached us without quite understanding why we had stopped.

"We were waiting for you! You're like a tortoise! Fancy a bit of wine?"

Lois gazed at us in surprise. Couldn't understand a thing. As if nobody had ever waited for him. As if the best he'd received was a beating. A kick in the stomach as you catch your breath. A fist making contact with your cheek. He grabbed the wineskin and took a swig. Then smiled at us. Wiped his red lips.

"We have to climb this hill. Then there's a short descent. The caves are behind the brambles and undergrowth. We'd better hurry. The weather is getting worse," warned Santiago.

We walked up the steep slope. The sky threatened a storm. Bolts of lightning could be seen in the distance. White lines. Light.

The Boulders were a group of three enormous rocks eroded by water and the passage of time. They were almost on top of the forest. Others call them the *Altar*. It's forbidden to call them that. They say it was a place of sacrifice in the pagan religion. The fact is it didn't look much like an altar. The rocks were round. The biggest was in the middle, the other two on either side. Truth is, with a bit of imagination, the Boulders looked like three human figures. A fat old woman with big breasts accompanied by two fat daughters. The three of them with closed eyes. As Santiago had said, it was full of undergrowth. Brambles. He removed the sickle hanging on his back and started cutting. Lois did the same.

"The entrance is this way. There's a cave between two rocks that goes underground," indicated Santiago.

"U... u... under... underground. Yyyyyyy... yes," repeated the Stutterer.

I prepared a torch so we could see in the dark. The storm was already over our heads. The rain returned. Fell on the forest. The trees. The ground. The corpses of ochre leaves. Gorse. Lois trembled. He was afraid of lightning. There was a whole heap of stories about Lois' stammer. Some said he became like that because when he was little a bolt landed on top of him in the cradle. That was why he found it so difficult to pronounce words with his tongue. What nonsense. Others, that he was frightened by the *Kranoraçem*, a forest spirit that can enter dreams and turn them into nightmares. Legends told by grandmas to frighten children. I wish the causes of Lois' stammer were those – that way, his story would be less tragic and more exotic. Mysterious.

The entrance to the Boulders was narrow. We had to go in sideways. The torch lit up the cave. There was a lot of dampness. The walls had imperfect drawings of men hunting some kind of animal. They looked like roe deer. Santiago opened his mouth. Lois as well, without forgetting the thunder reverberating outside. He was trembling with fear.

"Who do you think did this, sir?" asked Santiago, pointing at the drawings. He then made the sign of the cross.

"Somebody who was here before you. Before us. Before all this."

"*G… G… G… God*?" asked Lois.

I couldn't help smiling.

"I don't think so."

Suddenly the roar of a creature came out of the darkness that hadn't been dissipated by the torch. Brrrrrrrrrrrrrrrrrrrrrrrrrrrrrrrrrrrrrrrrrrr… We all went as stiff as stone statues. The light revealed a hairy head which opened its mouth and let out this enormous shout that echoed around the cave.

"A… a… a… bear!"

## LIFT THE FLESH DOOR

I heard their voices burning. Again. I gazed at them with indifference. Again. And they burnt. Again. All of them. Absolutely all of them. I didn't care then. And I don't care now.

Lois the Stutterer screamed as if he were being flayed alive. The doctor quickly stitched his wounds. He was losing lots of blood. Santiago had him pinned by the arms. Me, by the legs. He moved like a man possessed, as if a spirit had got inside his body. And screamed. Screamed without stuttering at all. Screamed loud and hard. Freely. Screamed in agony. Let it all out.

It hadn't been the wolf waiting behind that darkness. The bear. A bear. Brown. Big. Hairy. Santiago tried to leave quickly, but tumbled onto the ground. Lois was paralyzed by fear. The bear reared up and swiped him with a paw. The Stutterer was knocked unconscious. His face covered in blood. The bear dragged him to his part of the cave. Santiago let out a weak, tiny "noooooooooooo!!!"

"How did you do it, sir?" asked Santiago.

"What?"

"Ho... ho... how did you do it? How did you get Lois out of there. The... the... the... bear didn't touch you. Not you. Not at all. It just stared at you. And you stared back," Santiago's finger prodded me in the chest. "I don't... I don't understand."

"There's nothing to understand, Santiago. Go home. Rest. Hug your child. Your wife. And pray to *God* for Lois. These days are going to be long."

"And... where are you going, sir?"

"Me?" I asked in surprise. "Where do you think? To the tavern!"

Headbreaker was a curious nickname, even though it had its logic. Needless to say. Everything has its logic. It came from his grandfather. He always carried an oak stick with a metal ball at the end. The old man called it the *liquidator*. He was responsible for slaughtering the pigs on St Martin's Day. How did he do this? By whacking the pig over the head with his *liquidator*. The pig would fall down dead. "They were killed instantly. With a single blow. Can you imagine? He never missed once. It was quite a spectacle in the Valley." Ulfe Headbreaker told his grandfather's story with a sense of fascination. When he came to open the door of the tavern, he offered me a table on my own. Kicked off four men who had been playing dice. "Off you go! Come on with you! To another table! This man is a soldier of the *Queen*. A hero." Ulfe was a devoted follower of the *Queen* and the *Kingdom*. A sentiment inherited from his family. At the time of the peasant revolt in the Valley, his grandfather Headbreaker fought for Diogo de Guimaraes, the present Count's father. "And he broke lots of those wretches' heads with his *liquidator*." Many died in the *Revolt of the Sickles*, as it is called; others were exiled to the village of Slaughter, located at one end of the Valley, where the land is made up of sand and stone.

Headbreaker's was the only tavern in Valley Village. They had a good wine brought by a trader from the south. They also made this delicious pork-rib stew.

Ulfe Headbreaker served me a bowl of wine. "This one's on the house." I raised my bowl as a sign of gratitude. If Headbreaker had known how much I detest the *Queen* and all her sycophants, he wouldn't have been so kind to me. All the same, you have to make the most of these tiny gestures of generosity. Generosity is hard to come by in these parts.

The Collector entered the tavern. He was accompanied by another two men. The Alvariz twins. His lapdogs. The Collector's presence stifled the atmosphere. The voices, shouts, hullabaloo, gestures... quietened down. Headbreaker served the Collector and his minions very attentively.

"The usual, Collector?" asked Headbreaker, turning red.

"What did you call him?" demanded one of the twins brusquely.

"Ex... ex... excuse me. It... It... it was without thinking. It ju... it just came out!"

"Without thinking?" he pulled out a knife. "I might just kill you without thinking," the twin continued.

"Bu... but... I... I'm on your side!" Headbreaker gazed at the Collector with moist eyes. "My lord de Brandeso, you know how much I admire you and the Count."

Nunno de Brandeso, better known as the Collector, a nickname he hates, raised a hand in order to suppress the Alvariz twins' threatening language. Headbreaker served them three wines hastily. Anxiously. They drank them down and gestured to him to serve another round. The Collector leant on his elbow and glanced around. A slow, circular look. With enough time to take in the details. He stopped when he got to me. Took a deep swig of wine. Let out air through his nostrils in the bowl as he was swallowing. And carried on fixing me with his stare. A seemingly threatening look. He raised his eyebrows. Greeted me. I did the same. Silence descended between us like a rest. A truce. The Collector turned around and muttered something to the Alvariz twins. They swallowed the last drop of wine in their bowls and left.

When the door closed, the atmosphere increased in volume again. Shouts. Voices arguing. Voices chatting with abrupt gestures. Tobacco smoke cloaking the tavern in a grey mist.

There, on one's own, one thinks about one's things. It's inevitable. I thought about the *jungle*. White Cliffs.

Luiçiana. I thought about the wolf. About her. I thought about death. Him. About life.

Immersed in this bubble, at a distance from everything around me, I glimpsed a boy carrying a jug in his hand and serving wine. He worked in the tavern. He had dark skin and elongated eyes. He looked like a native. He also looked lacking in enthusiasm. I was surprised. Here? In the Valley? When he passed next to me, I grabbed him by the arm.

"Where are you from, eh?"

The boy struggled to get free. Emitted complaints. "Mmmmmrrrmmmrrrrrrrrrrr." I let go of him. Headbreaker was watching from the bar. When the boy came alongside him, he shouted at him. Gave him a clip around the ear. Sent him to the kitchen. I raised my hand and gestured to Headbreaker to come over. He grabbed the jug the boy had left on the counter. Walked quickly, avoiding the customers.

"More wine, sir?"

"No. I have enough for now. The boy, where's he from?"

Headbreaker took out a handkerchief. Wiped his forehead. Dried his sweaty hands.

"The boy? Did he do something, sir? Did he bother you?"

"No. He didn't do anything. He doesn't look like he's from the Valley."

"He isn't, milord. He's a native."

"A native?"

"Yes. Old de Souza brought him back from the *Americas*. They say he was his son. He got one of those

Indian women pregnant. Nobody believed it because he was very old. You know?"

"And where is this man de Souza?"

"Underground. He turned up dead on the farm he had in Suebi. The *Queen* granted him a piece of land for fighting for the crown and all that. The Count wasn't happy because the lands were his property. There were lots of quarrels between them. You see? The boy hasn't uttered a word since then. He's a rebellious type. Difficult to get on with."

"I understand. What's he called?"

"People around here call him the *Indian*. But his name's Tarthai."

And suddenly my heart exploded from the pain of hearing that name. Pain. Memory.

## LIP WAS NOT THE LIAR

Rain moistened the recently dug tomb of Lois the Stutterer. The priest, all dressed in black, carried an enormous silver cross in his hand. Lois' cross was wooden. And there was no name carved on it. Nothing. He will be an insignificant man whom no one will remember in a couple of years. Even Santiago will forget his friend. We will all forget. We will wonder whether Lois the Stutterer ever existed or it's just a diluted memory on a horribly rainy day. Like the mist. Inexistence. Then his body will have been completely swallowed up by the acidic rain. By the worms. By everything that makes us disappear down there.

There was only a gorse branch without any yellow flowers. A dry gorse branch. Dead. As dead as Lois.

"People are starting to talk, Mr d'Ourantes," said Coralia as she peeled potatoes with her knife. "It's a wood demon. Of the kind pagans worship. A devil seeking human souls. Apparently a girl from the village of Lower Town saw it. I heard this the other day on coming out of Mass. It appeared to her on the way to Royal Mill. She was carrying a sack of maize to grind at the Count's mills. Apparently it looked like a child and was naked. With red, cropped hair. And no eyes!" Coralia let go of the knife and made the sign of the cross three times. "No mouth!" Again. "No nose!" Almost the last. "And no face, either!" The last one, finally.

"What happened after that?" I asked with a hint of irony.

"Well, the girl from Lower Town – I don't know if it was Lower Town or St Eugenia, anyway, it doesn't matter – the girl got frightened. Who wouldn't? But a miracle took place. The work of the Virgin or our Lord. Who else? The pine she had lit to find her way at night let out a tall, brightly coloured flame. Like the bonfires on St John's Eve. And the demon – I told you the demon looked like a child, didn't I? Yes, I told you that... well, the demon transformed into a snake and slithered away through the undergrowth. I pray to *God* not to come across it one day, it would give me the heebie-jeebies!" Another three crosses.

"So now we're after a snake. I see..."

Each town has hundreds of stories. Men and women who encounter mysterious creatures. Always at night. Full moon. Storms. And suddenly a miracle. "*God*, the Virgin, our Lord..." Superstitions. That's why

I like Luiçiana. Ever since they got rid of the Church, they haven't had time for such nonsense. They know full well what lives in their woods. And they're afraid of the creatures. They hide behind locked doors on winter nights. The rain beats against the wood. They try to go out as little as possible. The bare minimum.

I went to the bedroom. I was prepared to spend the whole night in the wood. I was also ready to jump ship. To leave the Valley and go back to Luiçiana. The wolf wasn't my problem. It was the Count's problem. I'm no longer made for this sort of thing. The years weigh heavily on my body. My arms. My legs. My soul. My bones. On my memory.

The bedroom door was half open. I opened it fully. Heard a tiny murmur. Sniffling. In a corner, sitting on the floor, was the girl who helps Coralia in the kitchen. She was crying. Wearing a white nightdress with blood on the lower part. When she saw me, she became nervous. Tried quickly to stand up. Couldn't. Fell back down. And started crying again.

"What happened?"

She turned away. As if she found me repulsive. Tears coursed down her cheeks like a funeral procession. Sad and slow.

"Who did this to you?" I looked at the blood. "Who?"

She wept.

"Listen. I'm not going to hurt you. I promise," the girl was trembling with fear. Or cold. Perhaps both. "What happened?"

I got up. Took one of the blankets that had been neatly folded on the bed. They were made of wool from the Count's sheep. The nights are cold. Everything is cold here. I placed it carefully around her shoulders. The girl embraced the warmth, trembling as if a part of her anguish had disappeared at that moment. There was still the other part, though.

I took hold of one of her frail elbows. She tried to stand up. Gently does it. Looked pale. Sat on the bed. Tried to cover the bloodstain with her hands. Didn't stop crying. She had been abused. Raped. That much was clear. But by whom?

"Who did this to you?" I insisted.

She lowered her head in tears. Felt ashamed. She was a girl. She was frightened. I began to get angry because I could imagine the situation. I imagined her shouting and crying while someone pinned her down and tried to get inside her. War showed me some horrifying images. The *jungle* as well. I took part in those images. I was a protagonist. I used to be another person. I'm not like that anymore. But I did it. That's the worst sentence. Living with the memory.

The girl clung to the sheets. I sat down beside her. She let out a quivering sigh. Despite her white, seemingly cold skin, her body exuded burning heat.

"I'm not going to hurt you," I raised the palms of my hands. "I swear. What's your name?"

There was a moment devoted just to the two of us breathing. Inside the four walls. The stone. The space.

"Briana, milord," said this broken, childish voice.

"And what happened to you?"

She started crying again. Softly. Recalling the incident. Feelings that collapse like a house of cards. They don't stand up. Goose pimples. Trembling. Tears.

"I'm not a thief. It's just there's hunger. Lots of it," Briana spoke slowly, but didn't trip over her words. "Father and mother don't have anything to eat. I had to help them. That's why I go down to *master's* pantry. So they can have something to put in their mouths. Me too. *Master* has succulent dinners, but we go hungry. We. The people."

Briana swallowed air. Lots of it. Stared quietly at her wounded knees with their fresh, liquid blood. Then raised her eyes. Like someone getting up who's about to collapse on the ground once and for all. She looked at me.

"I went down slowly. Took a few potatoes. Flour. I wanted to take a piece of cake because it's my father's birthday the day after tomorrow. I was on the chair. Coralia always keeps the cake on the top shelf of the cupboard. Next to the butter and sugar. She doesn't ever give us any. I heard footsteps on the stairs. Crack! I thought it was Coralia. I quickly got off the chair and hid beneath the table. I was very frightened. And it was cold. I could only see their legs. There were two men. It was the Alvariz twins. As they talked, they grabbed things from the pantry. They drank. And ate. Said something about a plan. Bishop del Riego had arranged it all with the *Queen*. Constança would be part of a new bishopric because the Count didn't have an heir. 'It's all working out just as the bishop said it would,' they kept saying. I grew more anxious. 'Constança will belong to the Church.'

And they laughed out loud. A piece of bread fell on the floor. I gulped. When they bent down to pick it up, they discovered me under the table. They dragged me out like an animal on the way to slaughter. I screamed, but they covered my mouth. Then... then..." Briana started crying, "they did this to me," she looked at the blood on her nightdress. "The two of them, sir. The two of them. What will happen to me?"

The girl collapsed. Not physically. Physically she remained sitting on the bed with her hands covering her tear-soaked face. But inside, deep inside, everything was on the floor. Down on the floor. Never to be raised again. She was a girl. A girl. And she'd been raped by two men. Evil, wild men. Beasts.

"Are you sure about what you heard?"

She wiped the tears with her sleeve. Let out a sigh.

"Don't you believe me?"

"I didn't say that. I'm just asking if you're sure about what you heard beneath the table."

"Yes, I'm sure, sir."

"So how come you're here?"

She lifted her head.

"Because I got away. They were going to kill me. They were laughing. 'When this is over, you're dead, bitch.' They flung me on the floor," Briana's voice cracked, as if she was on her last legs. "I didn't have the strength to put up a fight. They placed me on my knees. And... and... I could see, beneath one of the cupboards, a knife. Gleaming. Sharp. I grabbed it with my hand. Closed my eyes. Swung around. Cut one of them on the hand. The other in the belly. They fell on the floor. Shouted out. I got up quickly. Knocked over the candle that lit the pantry. It went out. I heard them getting up and floundering around in the dark. 'Where are you going, bitch! We're going to kill you!' I raced up the stairs. Felt their breath behind me. Heard them cursing. I ran here as fast as I could. To your room. Hid. Hoping I wouldn't be discovered."

Briana fell asleep on the bed. I covered her frail body with the blanket. The Alvariz twins had branded her forever. A wound that will never stop bleeding. Eternal. Till the end of time. Perhaps the girl will never trust men again. She may even be afraid of them. She'll be left alone. She'll die alone. With no one at her side. And she'll pass through this world like a non-existent body. An insect. Nobody will ever name her. Like Lois the Stutterer, she will be extinguished.

But I have to admit I also thought about the other part. What she'd said. Or rather what the Alvariz twins had said. Bishop del Riego had arranged everything with the *Queen*. A new bishopric that would occupy the lands of Constança because the Count didn't have an heir. An heir.

## WHEN EVERYTHING THAT TICKED HAS STOPPED

The wood commands respect. Especially at these hours. In the half-shadows. The night.

The torch lit the path as if it was a sign of hope. But there is no hope in Constança. Santiago insisted on coming with me. I refused. I said I needed to be alone with the forest. I hoped to establish a connection. Like in the *jungle*. In the *jungle*, the savages called it "the link". When there is no ambiguity in nature and everything goes back to being a single form. A solitary piece. And man understands the *jungle's* language. And man is the *jungle*. And the *jungle* is man.

Silence. Nothing else. A terrible silence that foreshadows something even more terrible that is soon to come. There was no sound from the little owl. Nor from the boar crashing through the undergrowth. Nor from the insects on dry leaves or digging in the soil. From anything that persists in the depths and is invisible at night. Silence. Only silence. Terrifying.

The fire revealed some boulders that crossed each other. This time, they really did look like some kind of altar, the result of natural chance. But nothing's chance in this place. Some parts were covered in moss. I went over. On the stone that acted as a table, there was blood. Still fresh. There were also chicken feathers. I imagined some fox had tucked into a good dinner. The animal must have run away when it saw the light of the torch. Light. Fire. It could also have been some kind of pagan ritual in which a favour is sought from a god of the forest. The night is intense. Strong. Something starts to bother me. Step by step, my body feels an invisible, awkward pressure. The buzzing of a fly dynamites the silence behind my ear. The torch is blown out by an unexpected breeze.

Crack!

There's something there. Now, hidden behind the blackness. I remain motionless. Close my eyes. Try to perceive something more than the physical. To concentrate. The trees, around me. The forest. And the fire slowly comes back to life. Shows me the landscape again on this strange, mysterious night. Slowly. Very slowly.

Grrrrrrrrrrrrrrrrrrrrrrrrrrrrrrrrrrrrrrrrrrrrrrrrrrrrrrrrrrr!

In front of me, a grey figure that turns white. Walks. Four paws. Grrrrrrrrrrrrrrrrrr. The wolf! I grab hold of my knife. Grrrrrrrrrrrrrrrrr. It comes to a halt.

It's big. Its eyes, illuminated by the light of the torch, look red, but they're not, it's just an effect. I stay still. It doesn't stop looking at me. It licks its snout. Bares its teeth. Grrrrrrrrrrrrrrrrrrrrrrrrrrrr. They're white as well. Like its fur. I had never seen a white wolf. I found it beautiful, illuminated by the fire, like a celestial image. A painting. Grrrrrrrrrrrrrrrrrrrrrrr! It bent its back. Put one paw forward and crouched. Grrrrrrrrrrrrrrrrrrrrrr!! The wolf was ready to pounce. I didn't let go of the knife. I would have to be quick. Raise and stick it in at the precise moment. As it jumped.

Fiuuuuuuuuuuuuuuuuuuuuuuuuuuuuuuu!     Fiuuu! Fiuuuu! Fiuuuuuuuuuuuuuu!

Someone whistled behind the darkness. I could make out a human figure in the trees. Nothing else. A black, diluted figure that barely moved. After that rhythmic whistle, the wolf went back to its initial position, turned around, and headed towards that mysterious person. I stood there. Rigid. Immobile. I'd seen that before. In the *jungle*. Always the *jungle*. Petén hunters. That's what we called them. A tribe that settled in the Guatemalan jungle. The hunters took a black wolf with them. It reached their waists and had thick fur. Deep. Dark eyes. Taut, attentive body. The Petén hunters controlled the wolf by means of whistles. And the wolf obeyed. Moved to one side or the other depending on the rhythm and intensity. Attacked. Implacably. Quickly. Voraciously.

That scene took me aback. I hadn't been expecting to come across that in Constança. Not in this part of the world. Thinking about the *jungle*, those days, always diverts me from my existence. Thoughts do their own thing, and the body is just that – a body on its feet, without a soul, nobody controlling it on the inside.

"Who are you?" I shouted powerlessly. "Who are you?"

Nobody replied on the other side. Silence. Only silence. Terrifying.

# DAY KNOCKED AND WE MUST PART

"She stands accused of heresy and theft."

"She's just a girl," I groaned.

"Forgive me, Mr d'Ourantes, but don't make me laugh. At thirteen, she's not a girl anymore. She knows very well what she's doing."

"At least let her go before a court."

The bishop let out an ironic, unending guffaw that filled the empty space of the church. "Hahahahahahahahahahahaha.

"I told you not to make me laugh. I don't know how the world works out there, but here the only trial there will be is *God's*. And as our Lord's representative, I will pass sentence," exclaimed the bishop.

"She'll die in the flames. A girl of thirteen burnt at the stake. In the middle of Constança village square. Like some kind of spectacle."

Bishop del Riego stopped gazing at that altar full of celestial figures. Saints dressed in gold and silk, crosses, lit candles... Turned around. Pointed at me.

"I've heard the Supreme Pontiff holds your name in high esteem. The Pope has not forgotten what your family did for the Church. He's very grateful. The *Queen* also remembers. The great Captain Lourenço d'Ourantes!" he said mockingly. "Your legacy is so great it's become a sort of legend. It's so long we don't know if it was your grandfather, your father, or you yourself who performed the exploits that are recounted," he continued in the same tone. "That's nothing. A legacy, a story... it's a name. A surname. Ink on paper. D'Ourantes. Easy to delete. Easy to erase. And, above all, easy to tarnish. So be careful what you say. From hero to villain is a very short distance. Don't go against the word of our Lord because *God* won't have mercy."

Briana was imprisoned in the palace dungeons. She wasn't allowed any visits. She was going to be burnt the next day. At dusk. For everybody to see that lamentable image as a warning for those who espoused the old religion. The bishop, with complete impunity, wondered whether to have her crucified at the Gates of Holy Victory, to leave her body as a banquet for the crows. Sticking their yellow beaks in the putrefied flesh. Breaking the skin. Rotting flesh. In the end, he opted to have the girl burnt. So everyone could hear her screams of pain, which will completely destroy the serenity of the assembled crowd. Those screams will become embedded in their brains like needles. They'll turn into a nightmare. I know this well. I hear their voices burning. Burning the way they themselves burnt. In the flames. All of them. And I'll die with those shouts running loose inside me.

Off to the tavern. Again. Collapse on top of a bowl of wine, once more. Headbreaker's was full of people. It always is. Men. Drinking. Smoking. Everybody discussed the news out loud. "Tomorrow, one of the servants from the palace is going to be burnt. They say she's a kind of witch. She stole food from the pantry." Most of them nodded and made the sign of the cross when they heard that bit about "witch". A few dared to challenge the bishop's decision. Even so, they did it. Said they were fed up of the Church. "We work the lands of the Count and the Church, and what do we get in return? Misery!" Many people nodded. "Yeah, that's right. Misery!" Others issued warnings. "Be careful what you say."

I sat at an empty table. The Indian boy served me a bowl of wine. He looked unenthusiastic. As if he was angry with the world. He always wore that expression, eyebrows raised. He was very dark. Long, shiny, black hair. Men addressed him by the name of *Indian*. Raised their bowls so he would serve them another. And the boy, with his perpetual lethargy, served them without a word, while Headbreaker gathered up the coins they left in payment on the counter and stuffed them in his pocket.

Somebody sat down opposite. I didn't pay much attention. I was thinking about my things. You know. Recollections that can be like knives and affect your whole day. The harshness of memory. The odd good moment. Most, bad. And in that vicious, painful spiral, I looked up to bring myself back to reality. To my surprise, the person who'd sat at the table was the dwarf who had entered the House of the Viços, carrying a roe deer, while I chatted with Víctor. There he was, staring at me, not blinking. I did the same. Stared at him. We stayed like that for a good long while. And then suddenly…

"I told you, *Herr* d'Ourantes, one way or another, I would find out the end of the story."

The voice coming out of the dwarf's almost toothless mouth was the same as the *stranger's*. The same as Víctor F.'s. Exactly the same. I couldn't believe it. I jerked backwards.

"What sorcery is this?"

He smiled, and his smile had the selfsame form as those the *stranger* flashed me during our meeting at Snowy Peak. It was as if, despite having a dwarf with a pronounced beard, twisted nose, and dirty clothes in front of me, it was Víctor inside his dwarfish body. I couldn't understand.

"*Peter* was awaiting his execution in his cell," he took up the story where he had left it off in the House of the Viços. "It wasn't an iron cell. It was difficult to explain. A kind of dome made of branches and plants that came out of the ground. *Peter* was there, touching the branches, which moved slowly and blossomed in spring. Nature's prison. Zoriah had disappeared into the *jungle*. The Vermelhos hadn't heard from their chief in months. After carrying out the ritual of the dead and burying Tarthai beneath a tree, Zoriah performed what they call the *rest*, which is to mourn the death of a loved one in solitude, with only the deep *jungle* for company. The Vermelhos bury their dead among the roots of trees. They say the body has to nourish the *jungle*. The *jungle* is everybody's mother, you have to go back to her, to her belly. You understand, *Herr* d'Ourantes? You understand. Of course you do," he smiled. "The point is, in the end, Zoriah returned to the village and ordered the prisoner's release. Everybody was outside, making a circle. They placed *Peter* in the middle. Stripped him. Then Zoriah went over with a knife that had a mother-of-pearl handle," he stared at my belt. "Instead of executing him to avenge the death of his son, he gave him the knife as a sign of forgiveness. The Vermelhos' chief spared his life and accepted him into their community. Taught him to hunt. To speak their language. To understand the *jungle*. Taught him the *link*. To interpret nature. Trees. Animals. To converse with them. *Peter* understood the meaning of compassion and wept for all that he had done. He understood the pain brought about by wars, conquests, death, suffering, and felt released from it all. The Vermelhos gave him another name as a way of showing he had abandoned his past, the man he'd been and would never be again. His new name was Tolah. Time passed, and Tolah fell in love with Lizah, Zoriah's daughter. The chief blessed their union on a blue, starry night on which there were dances and rituals of eternal love. They had a child, named Tarthai in memory of her brother and Zoriah's son, whom Tolah, once *Peter*, had killed. But things don't stop there, *Herr* d'Ourantes, now is when it gets interesting. That's right," the dwarf took a swig of wine and grimaced. "Ugh! I hate wine. You don't know how to drink. If there's good beer, get rid of this bitter grape juice," he took another swig and fell silent. "There came a day when Tarthai was already a child on his way to becoming a strong, tall man. And suddenly, one night, when he was dining with his parents at the royal table, an arrow drove into his heart. Tarthai fell into Tolah's arms, in his death throes, and Tolah let out a shout that reached every vertex of the *jungle*, a shout just like the one Zoriah had let out when his son had been murdered. Burning with indescribable rage, Tolah looked up to see who had shot the deadly arrow that had killed his son. In the clearing in the *jungle*, where the Vermelhos perform their rituals of fire, Zoriah was standing with a bow in his hand. And all the Vermelhos, all of them, got up from the table and, little by little, walked until they were side by side with their chief. All of them. Even Lizah, who stood on her father's right. It had all been a trap threaded together year after year. They all knew what was going to happen. Zoriah. Lizah. Even Tarthai. They all knew the task they had to fulfil. Tolah walked with his dead son in his arms and placed him at Zoriah's feet. On his knees, in floods of tears, he asked Zoriah why he had done this. 'Why?' And Zoriah answered, 'Now you can imagine the pain I myself felt when you snatched away my son, *Peter*.' And then he uttered the curse. 'Until you feel the same sorrow, until you feel the same pain, you will wander this world without knowing death. You will see men turn to dust, moon after moon, sun after sun. Until you feel the same sorrow, until you feel the same pain.' Tolah stayed in the clearing, weeping on his knees for the death of Tarthai, who still had the arrow stuck in his chest, while all the others went back to their places to finish their dinner as if nothing had happened."

The dwarf fell silent. I grew tense. Behind the bar, the *Indian* washed the clay bowls without taking his eyes off me, with that accursed expression that was starting to annoy me.

"A very good story," I said impassively. "But I have better things to do than to sit here with you, listening to all that claptrap, Mr..."

"Call me Víctor."

I gazed at him with indifference.

"Víctor, right... Of course. I don't know what trickery this is. It's true, you mimic him very well, but take care, people around here confuse that kind of thing with matters of the devil, spirits, and witchcraft. I wouldn't want to see you hang at the Gates of Holy Victory."

I got up from the table and made as if to leave Headbreaker's.

"You know what that man's name was? You know *Peter's* real name?"

I stopped. Took a deep breath, as if it was my last.

"I'm not interested!" I shouted.

He didn't budge, and although we had our backs to each other – he was sitting down, and I was standing up –

I could imagine another of those smiles of his. Without showing his teeth. Without opening his mouth.

"Lourenço, Lourenço d'Ourantes. That was his name."

I left the tavern. Outside, it was raining pitilessly. Inside as well.

# I TAKE THEE BY THE HAND

When I opened the door, someone was waiting for me in the shadows.

I felt the blade on my neck. The imminence of death. The cold, sharp metal. How can such a simple tool be so powerful at such moments? One quick movement, and I would bleed to death on the floor. The delicate skin opens. The flesh, as well. If you focus your attention, you can even hear the sound it produces. Most people grab hold of their throats, as if wanting to stop the haemorrhaging. But there's nothing to stop. The blood runs out through their fingers, which are dyed red. And in the twinkling of an eye it's all over. Over.

One of the Alvariz twins was smiling. The one holding the knife as well, I imagine. I couldn't tell them apart. They were a copy of each other. An exact copy. The Collector didn't say anything. He was standing there in his long, dark overcoat and hat of the same colour, which went well together. I could even say he looked elegant.

"Truth is we had it in for you, Mr d'Ourantes," I felt the warm breath behind my ear.

The other twin hit me in the stomach. The Collector came over. He had green eyes. And a pronounced scar on his upper lip in the form of a "V". He took a breath. Let it all out in front of my nose. I didn't flinch. He went back to his initial position. Took out a small leather pouch. Rolled a cigarette. Lit a match. The flame hung there. A hypnotic orange colour. Fire. Burning. He lit the cigarette. Took a drag. The red light could be seen in that almost dark room. The rain beat against the floor. The roof. The leaves of the trees. Against anything that got in the way of its fatal fall.

"So it turns out you had a little chat with that whore we're going to burn tomorrow, is that right?" the breath on my neck again.

I didn't reply.

The twin in front of me smiled. Took a step forward. Our noses were almost touching. He was covered in spots. He had marks all over his face. I found him repulsive. Disgusting.

"Yeeeeeeeees... Hahahahahahaha!" he laughed manically. "Yes, you had a little chat. So what did she tell you? Eh?" he punched me in the chest.

I kept my lips closed.

He hit me in the stomach again. Harder, this time. I could feel it. I let out a whimper of complaint. "Ahhhhhhhhhhh!" My knees buckled. The one behind me lifted me up by the hair. The Collector was smoking. Like he had nothing to do with it. He just paced up and down the room.

"Let's see," continued the twin. "You tell us what the whore told you, and we'll let you go. You can go back to that shitty land of yours, all right?"

He adopted an expression like he was talking to a child. His breath reeked. It was obvious they were going to kill me, whatever I told them. And besides, I didn't want to tell them anything. I wasn't going to tell them anything. Because I was quite sure they were the ones who would tell me things. I started smiling without taking my eyes off the twin.

"What's so funny? Eh?"

I carried on smiling until I burst out laughing. "Hahahahahahahahahahaha!"

The twin turned around and looked at the Collector. Then at his brother, who pressed the blade harder against my neck.

"What the hell you laughing at?" said the voice behind my ear.

I took a breath.

"No... It's just... Buf! I was remembering what Briana told me, the one you call 'whore'. I just remembered something she told me about you and almost wet myself... I couldn't help it. It's just... whenever it comes back to me..."

"What the fuck did she tell you?" shouted the twin opposite me in a fury.

"Well… It seems, when you raped her, that's right, when you did that thing, the girl felt nothing at all. Nothing at all! And the poor unfortunate asked if that was because you had a willy that looked like a child's," the twins glanced at each other with raised eyebrows. "Tiny. Hahahaha! Since it was her first time, the poor unfortunate didn't know. Hahahahaha! She didn't know! And she didn't feel a thing! A thing!"

The twin behind me pushed me. The one in front kneed me in the stomach. They beat me in a corner of the room. The Collector was quiet and watched the scene. They didn't stop. I didn't defend myself. I endured the blows. Physical blows are nothing compared to mental ones. The ones inside your head. Inside. Wounds heal. They get better with time. In the end, there's a mark that will testify to a memory that will be carried on your skin until you die. But mental wounds are ever present. At all hours. As on the first day. Bloody. And they wear you out on the inside. They destroy you little by little. Sometimes you can't discern reality. Sometimes it's like a dream. A nightmare. The *jungle* is my wound. The curse.

My vision blurred as a result of the beating, I made out a knife coming towards me. The blade on my neck again.

"No!" shouted the Collector. "Not here. We'll do it outside. In the wood."

## TO FIND THE SUNRISE LEFT

There was a light breeze. Icy. Beating cruelly against my face. Cold. I had been tied to a wooden post. The rope squeezed my wrists. I was still confused. I could hear misshapen voices. The swaying branches of the trees, as they intermingled. The little owl at some inappreciable distance. Buuuuuuuu!!! Buuuuuuuu!!!

They give me a slap. Another. Harder. The image starts to become defined. The misshapen voices become clear. Linear.

"Eeeehhhhhh! You! Wake up!"

Once again, once more, one of the Alvariz twins. I recognized his voice. I could hardly see anything. Everything was very dark, poorly illuminated by a pair of torches stuck in the ground. A weak, yellow light.

Footsteps. Footsteps approaching slowly. Calmly. And a red dot that sometimes grows very intense. A cigarette. The Collector.

"Captain d'Ourantes," he began, "you know things you shouldn't," he took a deep drag and let out the smoke. "That's why we have to kill you. It's nothing personal, believe me," he came closer and looked at the ground. "Better do it here. In the wood," he gestured around with his hand. "You like the wood, don't you?" the twins smiled. "We'll make it look like the wolf killed you. You should know by now there is no wolf," he took another drag, and then another. "It's all a lie. A well devised plan." There was a silence. One, two, three... he continued, "It was us who killed the Count's son."

Even though my face showed no momentary surprise – something I found difficult to conceal – an icy shiver ran down my spine. They were the ones who'd killed the Count's son. Now I understood that bit about "working out as the bishop said it would". Of course, del Riego was behind this. Behind everything. But what was I doing there? "You know by now there is no wolf." And yet I'd seen the wolf. White. Taut. Strong. And someone with it. Controlling it.

"Constança Valley will fall to the Church. It will be called the Diocese of Holy Victory of Constança. What do you think?"

I didn't say anything.

The Collector gestured to one of the twins, who quickly came over and punched me in the stomach. Twice.

"Speak when you're spoken to!" he growled.

I swallowed air. Spat out the saliva that had gathered in my mouth. Next to my teeth. My tongue. In there.

"A very original name. Diocese of Holy Victory of Constança. But I doubt the other nobles and landowners will like it very much if the Church suddenly starts grabbing land by royal decree."

The Collector spat on the ground of night. Took another drag. Stuck a hand in his pocket.

"Listen, to tell the truth I couldn't care less what the other landowners think. Marquises, counts, landlords... It's all the same to me. The advisers to the *Queen* can resolve all of that. But let me tell you something else. When the Church starts ceding land to the peasants, who do you think they're going to support? Those hungry wretches have been ploughing a lord's property for centuries. To them, a piece of land will be like a chest of gold, captain. The Count doesn't have an heir. That's a problem. People are starting to believe the wolf is a curse. A devil. They won't go out. They're afraid. They pray to *God*. The Church must answer their prayers."

I was there. I had returned. I had a proper perspective. The confusion caused by the twins' beating had evanesced like morning mist. That mist that rises next to the river and disappears when the sky starts to open. I was there. Back *in situ*. Once again.

"So what do you get out of all this?" I asked.

The Collector continued to wear a serious expression, as if he was in the habit of keeping his emotions under control at all times. He seemed an unhappy man. With constant sorrow. Blackness. But the truth is that was his personality. A soulless piece of meat.

"Me? Nothing. I just do what they tell me. What they order me to do. When I've finished, I'll ship off to another place, with another mission under my arm. These little movements, Mr d'Ourantes, these imperceptible deeds, are what change the world. What shake it like a sheet hung out to dry. And after this, nothing will be the same. Sometimes an act that seems insignificant can have the most earth-shattering consequences."

The Collector was right. It's the little movements that put paid to everything. They're silent. Nobody discerns them, and suddenly there's a war and the established order is altered. Governments, systems, fall. Power changes hands. Everything begins with a spark, and then comes the fire that destroys everything. I don't know why the *Queen* allowed the Church to control Constança. Perhaps to get more power in the state after the loss of almost all the colonies in wars. Perhaps to keep the monarchy alive in the face of revolts in the capital. Or maybe it wasn't a movement of the *Queen's*. Maybe it was a movement of the Church's. But Constança doesn't have anything. It's a small valley with mountains and lands. A place people depart from. They abandon everything. Leave their stone houses from one day to the next with the table still set for lunch. They rush off to cities or ex-colonies.

"Who do you think governs, Mr d'Ourantes? Kings? Generals? Ministers? No. No, milord. Believe me when I tell you this, all of this," the Collector's gesture took in the surrounding landscape, "is not what it seems. The one who governs is not who we think. They don't have the power. Others have it," there was a seemingly short silence. "Have you heard of the *Executors*?"

The *Executors*. The first time I heard about them was in the hold of a ship. Outside, the storm was impenetrable. The ship was rocking like a cradle. In between those movements, wine and tobacco to calm the nerves, stories arise. Soldiers bond by holding conversations. In the cold, next to a fire, waiting for death... Perhaps we do this to hide our fear more than to cement ties. So someone will remember us after our death. Where we came from. What our first battle was. Who we fell in love with. Anecdotes. Village legends. Stories that spread from mouth to mouth. And in one of those situations, somebody makes mention of the *Executors*.

"Spies. Adepts. Solitary folk who follow orders from an organization that is the one that really directs the world from an island called *Olympus*," I caught my breath. "A very interesting, ancient legend. A legend."

The Collector revealed an almost imperceptible sign of satisfaction by means of a slight curvature of his lips. The poor imitation of a cynical smile. It may not have meant anything. A simple gesture lacking in emotion.

"Legends sometimes have shades of reality, Mr d'Ourantes. The *Executors* are given a mission. It can come to us in various ways. We don't know what the objective is. Our obligation is to complete the mission and not ask questions. To *execute*. We are trained for this from an early age. Small acts that have a greater purpose. All the revolutions the world has experienced were caused like that. They tell us what to do. We obey."

"Who are they?"

He gave me a penetrating look, the kind that pierces our flesh and sees what we have inside. The kind that hurts. He didn't say anything. He turned around. Raised an arm. The Alvariz twins came over. One was carrying a torch. It was so close I could feel the heat of the fire on my cheeks. The other was dragging a sack full of what looked like utensils.

"Are we going to do what we did to the boy?" one of the twins asked the other.

"We'll cut his throat, let him bleed, and then... Yum! Yum!"

They burst out laughing.

"You brought it, right?"

"What the fuck do you think is in this sack?" shouted one of them.

From the sack, they pulled out some kind of metal denture. It had these sharp iron teeth that fitted together like a pair of jaws. It was like a wolf's head made of iron.

"One question," I said. "Did you use that contraption to kill old Pelaiz as well?"

The twins smiled. The Collector continued with his back to me.

"Old Pelaiz had lots of enemies," he remarked. "He seemed like a nice enough fellow, but the son of a bitch was a collector," he finished the cigarette with a long drag, chucked it on the ground, and gestured to the twins to continue what they were doing.

"Right then. Lift his head."

One of the twins stood behind me. Grabbed my chin in both hands. I tried to resist, but, tied hands and feet, there wasn't much I could do except despair. The Collector watched from a distance. His figure merged with the darkness, creating a certain harmony. The cigarette's red end flared up... The smoke slowly clambered up his face. It was cold. Just like that night in the *jungle*. Everything burnt. They burnt. Them. Watching them, I felt cold.

One of the twins put a knife to my throat.

"*Bon voyage*, Lourenço d'Ourantes. If it was up to me, you wouldn't die so quickly. You'd suffer. You know what? When we've finished up here, we're going to visit the cell of that whore who told you everything. Yeah, that's right. We'll pay her a visit and have us a fun time. You understand, right? Then tomorrow she'll burn on the pyre. Just imagine how the little bitch will cry out."

Grrrrrrrrrrrrrrrrrrrrrrrrrrrrrrrrrrrrrrrrrrrrrrrrrrrrrr rrrrrrrrrr!!!! The sound came from behind the blackness of the wood. The twins went rigid. Motionless. Looked around. Grrrrrrrrrrrrrrrrrrrrrrrrrrrrrrrrrrrrrr!! The Collector took hold of a firearm he carried on his belt. Grrrrrrrrrrrrrrrrrrrrrrrrrrrrrrrrrrrrr!!

"What the fuck is that?" shouted the twin who was behind me. "Cut his neck, why don't you!"

The white wolf jumped out of the darkness onto the twin holding the blade of the knife to my throat. Tore off his arm. The twin shouted out, gazing at the empty space that had been left by what had once been a limb. "Ahhhhhhhhhhh!!!" The wolf carefully deposited the arm on the ground and attacked him again. Bit his face this time. The blood stained the twin's dirty shirt a red colour. He was choking in his own blood, his eyes wide open. It was coming out through his mouth. I was in a privileged position to watch this terrifying (but also beautiful) scene. The body expiring. The wolf turned around. Big. Strong. Wondrously taut. Bared its teeth. Grrrrrrrrrrrrrrrrrrrrrrrr!! I didn't move a finger. I was still tied hands and feet to that blasted post. I could hear the ragged breathing of the other twin, who was still right behind me. I couldn't see his face, but I could feel his warm breath. I suppose it was one of those moments when the situation is too much for you and you don't know what to do. You stand there, not moving. Defeated. Weak. Trapped in a nightmare. Hoping to wake up soon. But you never wake up. It's all too quick. Or slow. The wolf took a step forwards. Then another. Grrrrrrrrrrrrrrrrrrrrrrrr!! Attacked again. Passed next to me. Brushing against my knees. All I could hear was the other twin's screams of pain. Hair-raising. I envisaged the image. Booom! The Collector fired and fled into the belly of the forest. The wolf passed next to me again, in hot pursuit. While I had the corpse of the first twin laid out in front of me, the other was in his death throes at my back. It seemed he wanted to say something. He couldn't put together the requisite words. He let out laments full of air and indecipherable phrases until silence closed his mouth. Death. And in that picture where I was surrounded by two corpses, the immensity of the wood all around me.

# THE WATERS WRECKED THE SKY

It wasn't difficult to get free. After all the tension, the sweat did its thing. The rope loosened, and I was able to free myself with a bit of work. The twins' bodies lay on the ground. I could hear flies buzzing around them. Tomorrow, they won't be here. The creatures of the forest will come and feed on them. They'll smell the blood and find themselves a banquet of human flesh. It's strange. They look like two men in the full ecstasy of sleep. Having a nap. Like children sleeping in the most extravagant postures. One without an arm. The other without half his neck.

I rushed towards the palace. Crossing the darkness of the wood on narrow paths. It's a calm night. With a full moon obscured occasionally by some cloud. I don't like it. It doesn't do justice to the way things turned out. The night should not have so much serenity. It should be an agitated night. A night on which people died. Red. Bloody. I thought I might bump into the wolf. Or the Collector's corpse, missing some part of his body, among the trees. But the only thing I came across was the blackness that already travels with me. Ever since the *jungle*. Blackness. Always. The *jungle*. Always, as well.

I entered through the back gardens of the palace without making a noise. The door was locked. I needed to get down to the dungeons. There's no one on watch. Not anymore. It's an impromptu prison. The detained are shut behind iron bars. Given a bowl of soup and a crust of bread in the morning. The same in the evening. Days later, they are taken to court on a cart. Briana was going to be burnt at dusk without a trial, by order of the bishop. She would die on a pyre at the age of thirteen. It would be a spectacle everyone would view as an act of justice. Many others would watch on with horror, but even so, they wouldn't take their eyes off the appalling image. It would be hypnotizing. The fire. The burning body. The shouts caught up in the flames. I couldn't let this happen.

Opening a locked door has its difficulties, but it's easier than you think. After so much time, it's easy to do things other people find complicated. Impossible at times. Nothing is impossible.

I walked down the palace corridors, trailing my fingertips along the walls. There's hardly any light. Hardly any at all. Not just here. In this world. In this world, there's hardly any light. Hardly any hope. In the *jungle*, everything irradiated light. Stepping on the ground with bare feet. Running through the forest. Gazing at the branches of trees from below. The long, unending trunks. The transparent water in the river. Catching a fish with your hands. Children's smiles bursting in the air. Rays illuminating the leaves. Unexpected rain falling on your face.

The steps are narrow. It's like a spiral staircase. Going down. How much silence there is here. How much silence there is in Constança. In its people with their sealed lips. Women in mourning. Men worn out by ploughing the land. Skeletal. Wrinkled skin despite their youth. They're old at the age of twenty. Perhaps they're born old. I can picture the scene. The mother, young but old, opening her legs, pushing with pain and the sweat that runs over her aged body like a stream. From between her legs comes a newborn but old baby, who will continue in the tradition of working a land that will never belong to them. Their lives are a circle. A wheel going round and round and round... Everything on repeat, the same, generation after generation, until this world is consumed in flames.

It's cold in the dungeons. Water everywhere. I have to admit I've seen worse ones. There are no guards here to mistreat you or piss on you. The floor is made of stone. Aurora is responsible for bringing down the food and giving it to them under the door. People aren't normally kept here. Only exceptional cases, like Briana. Even so, since del Riego came to power, there've been a few. All of them pagans who conspired against the Church. At the time of the revolt, the cells were chock-a-block with prisoners, even though most of the rebels were put to death on the same day. Hanged at the Gates of Holy Victory. Like the pagan family swinging on the day of my arrival in the Valley. Others had a limb cut off. Or were tortured. Depending on the case.

"I knew you would come. It was logical."

Inside the cell, Briana was not alone. The Collector held a knife to her throat. She was pale. A real mess. In a white nightdress that had been stitched up all over the place. The same nightdress that had blood lower down. It was as if they'd gone into her bedroom in the middle of the night, grabbed her by the hair, and dragged her there with as much brutality as possible. That may have been what happened. She was crying with her head down.

"I thought the wolf had got you," I said.

The Collector smiled. He didn't look too good himself, albeit he was still firm and impenetrable. Made of metal. But he couldn't hide the fact he'd had a difficult night trying to escape the clutches of a wolf.

"Almost. But not quite. How do you do it?"

"What?" I replied uncertainly. I didn't know what this question referred to.

"As I fled through the wood, I could hear the wolf crashing through the forest behind me. But there was someone else with it. A dark silhouette running alongside, whistling as if communicating with the animal. You understand?"

"You think that was me?" I asked in disappointment. "Wow! I thought you were more intelligent – or have you forgotten you tied me to a post?"

The Collector spat on the floor. Sweat ran from behind his ears. His cheeks were red.

"I don't know. There are lots of stories about you. Rumours."

I raised my eyebrows.

"Such as?" I asked mockingly.

Silence.

"Some say your father sold you to mercenaries in payment of a debt," continued the Collector. "Others assert you were never a captain or a member of the troops. You're a phoney who trained wild dogs to attack villages so they would hire you as a wolf hunter – that is until things got out of hand in White Cliffs."

I became serious. Expelled all the air. Closed my eyes. I didn't want to remember. But memory got there first and showed me the images inside my head. That overcast day. The delicate wind combing the field. The standing cross. The trail of blood on the road. Children lying in the dry grass like rag dolls. White Cliffs.

"On the other hand," he continued, "there are those who maintain you're a hero. A great soldier. Brave. Cruel. Bloody. Very loyal to the *Kingdom* and to *God*. They say you're older than you look. You talk to animals. Fornicate with them. But my favourite, without a doubt, is the one that says you can't die. You've been walking in this world for centuries. You were cursed by a lost tribe in the *Americas* whose prisoner you were during the *Kingdom's* first expeditions. Like I said... rumours."

"Rumours... If only you knew! People are like that," I stuck out my tongue and showed it to him. "They have lots of imagination."

My heart started beating rapidly. Boom boom boom boom boom boom boom! I hadn't been expecting the Collector to be in the cell with Briana, and that had had an effect on me. I have to admit I'd thought it was all going to be easier. The twins dead, the Collector lost in the wood, trying to keep his bottom from being gnashed by a wolf. And yet here he was again, right in front of me, like a ghost. I started thinking of a plan to save the girl, but in none of them did things end well.

"What are you doing here?"

I wanted to know what the Collector was about. To find out if there was a crack in that seemingly impenetrable figure. The tiniest hint of goodness.

"I'm finishing the mission, Mr d'Ourantes."

"The mission? You have to make sure she dies?" I pointed at Briana. "What's a thirteen-year-old girl got to do with all this?"

The Collector kept smiling. Didn't take his knife off Briana's neck. She lifted her head. Hair partially covered her face. She was still crying.

"Her?" said the Collector. "No, Mr d'Ourantes. Not her. She will burn tomorrow. You. You are the one who must die."

Briana took a step forwards, pushed by the Collector. They were still in the same position. He with a knife threatening to cut her skin. She, terrified. They came out of the cell.

The Collector took the firearm from his belt. In one hand, the knife in the same posture. In the other, the firearm aiming at me. All held together by those elegant black leather gloves. I raised my hands as a sign of surrender. It seemed all I needed to do now was beg.

"I suggest a deal. Do with me whatever you like. I'm all yours. But save the girl. She doesn't have to die. Help her escape. Take her to some nearby village. Say it was me who did it, and that is why you had to kill me. She's only a girl."

Silence descended on the dungeons, the same silence there had been before our arrival. A silence that has been there for years, keeping the prisoners company in their iron cells. Their isolation between stone walls. Memory before it went *God knows where*. A silence in which there is only oneself and one's thoughts.

"No. I can't leave any loose ends. Things must happen like this. That's what they said. I'm following orders, Mr d'Ourantes."

Booooooooooooooooooom!

The Collector fired. And the silence vanished in the smoke from the barrel.

## PEACE BY ITS BATTLES TOLD

I watched them. Burning. All of them. All of it. Burning. And I wasn't sorry.

I felt the lead bullet passing through my body. Damaging everything we have in there. I felt the blood pouring out. My stomach burning. I let out a deep-seated cry. A lament. It bounced off the walls of the dungeon like a final farewell. The last word. Indecipherable.

I was on the floor, clutching my wound with my hands. It's an automatic gesture. It hurts. I feel the pain. The pain is part of the curse. The pain is there. It lasts a moment, but it's intense. It was the first time I'd been shot at such close range. From where I was, I could see Briana's bare feet. Behind, the Collector's boots.

I lifted my head. Stared at them from below. They maintained the same posture. The knife. Her throat. A girl's tears. And pain filtering through an open wound.

I got up. Slowly. Those moments when you talk to yourself. Come on. All right now. Up you get. Your will pushes you to achieve the impossible.

The Collector was still aiming at me, but his arm wasn't so firm or rigid anymore. Like he wasn't all that sure about my movements. Like he was amazed.

"Shit!" I shouted.

I tore my blood-soaked shirt, still complaining. The pain. The pain is part of the curse. The pain is always there. My torso was bare. Naked in that damp, underground place.

I looked at Briana. The Collector. The floor. Then again, Briana and the Collector.

I put my fingers inside the wound caused by the bullet. Right inside. I made an effort. Deep down. Descended into the universe contained by my body. Muscle. Guts.

"Ahhhhhhhhhhhhhhhhhhhhhhhhhhhh!!" I shouted louder this time. Pain. Pain. Pain.

Briana fainted in the Collector's arms. He let her fall to the floor. He still had the barrel pointing towards me, but his face wasn't so impenetrable anymore. His eyebrows were raised. His mouth, open. He was motionless, and straight away I saw a hint of fear in that gesture.

Slowly, I pulled my fingers out of the belly of the wound. Shouted again. It's inevitable. The pain. Always. "Ahhhhhhhhhhhhhhhhh!! *Goooooooooooood*!!"

I managed to extract the bullet. Circular. I looked at it. Blew on it. Stood up straight. Erect. Calm down. That's it now. All over. I dropped it on the ground. It sank into the blood turning the stone red.

The wound started closing by itself. The flesh rejoined. Formed a scar in seconds. And the blood stopped. The pain diminished. The Collector's eyes were as big as saucers. He was so taken aback by that image that the firearm slipped from his fingers and landed on Briana's prostrate body. Now he looked like a weak man. Frightened. The Collector was a cockroach about to be crushed underfoot. Crack!

"How... how did you... That's... sorcery... Things of the... Devil. How did... the bullet... the wound... heal... heal itself... How did you do that?" the words stuttered out of his mouth.

I went over to him.

"Now you know which of the rumours is true, Collector."

I took out the knife, which since the *jungle* had been untouched by blood. Since the *jungle*, it hadn't pierced human flesh. I stuck it in him. Right inside. With the rage of wanting to pass right through his body. He didn't defend himself, he just looked at me as if searching for answers. He slumped to the ground, letting out a breath that would be his last.

I took Briana. Carried her in my arms. She was still unconscious. Her hair, soaked in blood. Her nightdress, as well. I don't know if it was mine, the Collector's, a result of the twins' abuse or the blow she had received when she fainted.

I left the dungeon, gathering pace. In the dark. We had to get out of there before someone appeared and discovered the scene. I had to get Briana out of Valley Village as quickly as possible. The first light of day would soon pass through the mountains. They would go down to fetch her so she could be burnt at the stake prepared for her in the square. They would go down, but they would find someone else in the cell.

# TO SEE THE SUMMER SKY IS POETRY

She carried on crying.

"Listen to me!" I screamed, glancing around. "Listen," I repeated more softly. "You have to go on your own. It's dangerous, but you have to do it. Hurry while it's still dark. We don't have much time. You have to follow the road to Slaughter. Nobody will harm you there. They all hate the Count and the bishop. There's an inn. Ask for it by the name of *Sickles*. Wait there. Trust me. I'll come and find you."

"But... Why don't you come with me? I... I... I'm afraid."

"You have to go on your own. Don't you see? I have to sort a couple of things out here," I took hold of her cheeks. "Listen, you have to take a risk. That's life for you. Risky. You have to reach Slaughter. That's better than getting burnt in a fire, don't you think?"

Briana shed a tear which coursed down her pale face and fell, moistening the earth with salt. I got on the horse. She stood there, watching me leave. I was wearing the Collector's overcoat. It was cold. It was always cold. However much you wrap up, the mist filters through the gaps and freezes your bones. That's how it feels.

I had to find the wolf. I had to know who was travelling with it and controlling it. That can't be learnt here. Or it can. I don't know. Perhaps it was the *Eadar* who found me after I came down from Snowy Peak. She had got inside my body. I felt her rummaging in my insides, making things from the past rise to the surface. The followers of the old religion have gods that belong to the wood. Trees. Wind. River water. Rain. They worship animals. Deer. Snake. Bear. Wolf. They say the old druids had certain powers when they were in their sacred wood. There are lots of stories about that. They performed rituals to ensure good harvests. I don't know. In the *jungle*, I saw things you wouldn't believe. I was there. I was part of them. I felt them. But here everything's dead. People stopped seeking favours from the gods of nature centuries ago. Now they go to church and pray to the One *God* or the Virgin.

It was necessary to go back to the place where I'd been tied up by the Collector and the Alvariz twins. There where the wolf appeared for the last time. White. Strong. I had to try to make the *link*, as Zoriah had taught me in the *jungle*. To understand nature's language. There, the wood was alive and radiant, it filtered through the veins of my body. I could hear voices in my brain, as if I was just another component. We were a single entity. Here, everything's dead. It contains hatred. Resentment. Seems to be infected. A poison in the form of mist.

The twins' bodies were not there. They had disappeared without a trace. All that was left was a bloodstain on the grass. A scrap of shirt. Two boots from the same foot. And the wooden post I'd been tied to.

I got off the horse. Went barefoot. Closed my eyes. Tried to concentrate so I could see where the wolf had gone to. It had pursued the Collector through the forest. But it hadn't hunted him down. Where did it go? Who is the one that goes with it?

I felt the grass under my feet. The greenness. I walked. Touched the trunks of trees. They were like an old person's skin. Something impelled me to go in a certain direction. A voice murmuring inside my head. A woman's voice in an unknown language I could barely decipher. But still I walked, and at a certain point I saw a light in the wood which dispelled the poison in the form of mist. Everything was clearer. More shiny and exact. I could smell the wolf. Smell its trail like an imaginary line that dodged trees and everything that got in its way.

By the time I realized, dawn had started to break. Bringing rain. Another shitty day. Everything had gone back to the way it was before. Been extinguished once more. Back to the poison.

I had reached a marshy, muddy place. The wolf's paws had sunk in. I could see its prints. It had left a well-marked trail. I followed in its footsteps. Slowly. Easy does it. The clarity was warm and weak. The day, overcast. The rain started falling more heavily, the mist was intense. I ground to a halt. There was nothing left to follow. Nowhere to go. The prints in the mud had vanished as a result of the downpour. Which was getting stronger all the time. I looked around. I didn't know what place this was. I'd been going round in circles for some time. Hours even. I was lost. The wood had come to an end. In front of me was a mountain with three rocky peaks. Although it seemed far away, I could make out three settlements on top.

"Hey! You!" a distant shout.

I turned around. Behind the mist, I glimpsed the figure of a man.

I went over. There was a little stone house with a thatched roof. In the entrance, protected from the rain, an old man with a woollen blanket on his head.

"Take shelter, man! Come over here!" he cried, raising his hands.

I approached the old man. Suddenly, from the mist, there appeared a pair of horns. A cow, which went around me. Two steps further on, another cow was chewing the cud. I lifted my arms to shoo it away. The cow looked at me and carried on slowly wherever it was going.

I stood next to the old man in the entrance to that stone house with its dilapidated roof.

"You're barefoot!" he pointed at my feet. "You're going to catch a cold! You can't walk around like that, you have to wrap up. Wrap up warm. That's right."

The old man leant on a long stick. He shouted when he spoke, as if the rest of the world was deaf. Though most probably he was the deaf one. His voice was high-pitched. He had these small, sunken, black eyes. Despite wearing lots of clothes, he was a short, thin man. His skin was pale and wrinkled. His hands were chapped.

He laid the woollen blanket he'd been wearing on his head over my shoulders. This gesture revealed a bald patch.

"It's not necessary, sir," I said.

"Yes, it is. I've got too much on," he replied, arranging the blanket so it would cover as much of me as possible.

"Where am I?"

The old man looked at me and scratched his neck.

"You're at the *limits*, sir. This is where Constança Valley ends."

"And those three villages there, what are they?" I pointed in the direction of the mountain.

The old man scrunched up his eyes. Put the palm of his hand over his eyebrows like the peak of a cap, as if this gesture would enable him to see better. He indicated the mountain with his stick.

"That... They're not villages... Villages like nowadays, you know? Those are *castros*. It's called Three Castros Peak. That's supposed to be where the three *clans* who settled these lands lived. Before all this became Constança. Listen, that one there is called Anxeiriz," he showed me the left one with his stick. "That one's Bieiriz," he showed me the middle one, "and the other is Outeiriz," the right one. "They're abandoned. They've been like that for years. They were repopulated by villagers from outside, though I can't quite remember now. They always seem to me to have been in ruins. Stone, circular walls. Now they serve as a refuge to some shepherd or itinerant travellers. In fact…" he signalled with his stick again. "Look! There's smoke! There must be someone up there. You see?"

Through the gaps in the mist could be seen a grey line winding up to the sky, which was also grey. It was the smoke from a fire, lit on a hearth perhaps. It was coming from the *castro* the old man had called Bieiriz, the one in the middle.

The rain had decreased, though it was still weak and slow. The grass was wet. Around us could be heard the movement of cows. Mooooooooooooooooo! I couldn't work out how many there were. They emerged suddenly from the mist, like ghosts. Some of them had bells hanging around their necks. You could hear them. The old man gazed at the white infinite. A normal view for him, I suppose.

"You're a shepherd, right?" I asked.

"I am, sir."

"And these are your cows?"

The old man started laughing. He was missing teeth. He took out a handkerchief and wiped his face. Put it away again.

"If these cows were mine, sir, I'd be rich!" he carried on laughing. "No, sir, no. I'm a shepherd for the nobility of Clear Waters. Don't you know it?"

"Actually… no," I'd have liked to tell the old man I did, but the truth is I was unaware of that place.

He took me by the arm, and we walked a few paces forward. Pushing aside the mist with our hands. Pushing aside the cows that got in our way. The old man had a limp. He leant heavily on one leg, and then rested on the other. Half a smile hung off cracked lips.

"Listen," he said. "See that path that goes back into the wood?" I nodded. "Well, you go that way until you get to a crossroads. Then you follow a paved road. We call it Clear Waters Way. At the end of that, you reach the little town of Clear Waters, also known as the nobility of Clear Waters."

The old man always gave directions by pointing with his stick. It was as if he really travelled to the destination in his mind. He closed his eyes. Opened them. Closed them again. There were times he even made as if to take a step forwards. To put his feet on the road. To feel the earth beneath. The grass. Then the stones of the Way. And at the end, Clear Waters in front, with its walls of washed stone. The fountains spewing water. The roses blossoming in gardens. The nobles' houses. All cared for and strange.

"How many nobles are there in Clear Waters?"

"I have three *masters*. Three families. They cultivate wine. Make cheese. Milk. Meat. Wood. Skins. Trade in all of that. It used to belong to the clergy. The nobles administered it. But when the first revolt started, my *masters* took advantage. You know? The clergy hurried away, because apparently they'd burnt churches and hanged priests in other places. I don't know if that's true. The revolt never arrived," he scratched his head. "My *masters* proposed buying the lands that belonged to the Monastery, Clear Waters included. The clergy accepted."

"So... what are you doing here? These meadows belong to Constança Valley, don't they?"

The old man laughed. Took me by the arm. We turned around and went towards the little stone house to seek refuge from the rain.

"What am I doing here? Grazing the cows! What do you think? My *masters* have an agreement with the Count. Don't ask me what it is," he raised his arms. "I just do what they tell me. Clear Waters has few meadows. It's very mountainous. The vines are situated on the sides of canyons that follow the course of the river. They're like steps up the mountain. Difficult to reach. But the grapes grow well, and the wine is good quality."

We entered the house. There were sheep skins scattered on the floor, making a kind of bed, and the embers of a fire that had almost gone out, but still emitted warmth. On a stone, he had a knife stuck in a piece of cheese. Slices of bread around it, with crumbs. A bowl of milk. And half a chorizo.

"Did you spend the night here?"

"I did, sir."

"You didn't hear anything? See somebody going by?"

The old man grew tense. Glanced around. Leant on my arm. Sat on a stone. Sighed. Gazed at the dilapidated roof of the house. Then at his feet. He was wearing leather shoes. They were chestnut brown and very worn.

"Well, now that you say so, sir... I was lying here," he pointed to the sheep skins. "I always sleep with my eyes on the door. You can see what state it's in," the door was rotten and full of holes. "I heard this breathing next to it. An animal's sharp gasps. Saw this white skin through the gaps. And enormous teeth. I was afraid, sir. I felt fear. And I prayed to the Virgin. It went around the house. Once. Twice. Three times. It was as if it could smell me and wanted to pass through the stone walls. I didn't hear it after that. But the strange thing was that a few moments later I heard these footsteps on the grass. A body moving quickly. Going from side to side. Aimlessly. I thought they were going to come in. But they didn't. They went in the direction of the three *castros*. I'm almost sure of it. I felt really afraid."

The old man made the sign of the cross. Stared at the ground with his hands on the stick's handle. Moved his lips as if sucking something. Let out the odd "Ah!" and "Dearie, dearie me!" Then looked up and contemplated my face without saying anything. Sat there for a while, gazing silently at me. I could hear the rain hammering on the roof. It was pouring down again. The water was coming in. Forming droplets. He carried on sitting there. Pondering something in a mind with too many years, perhaps. Watching me. Until he dared to come out with it.

"You think it was a werewolf?" he asked.

## BLAZING IN GOLD
## AND QUENCHING IN PURPLE

The old man stood there as I left the *limits*. First, he showed me a shortcut to get to the three *castros*. "A shepherd's path." As I walked, I could picture the old man behind me. A stone figure. Following the wake until I was washed away from the landscape. Until the final moment. Still. In silence. With his stick on the ground as if it was holding up the world.

"You think it was a werewolf?" I carried that question in my mind on my journey to the three *castros*. Those are the facts that will later give rise to a legend. Everything happens like that. The confusion of words. Years later, the story of the werewolf of the *limits* will be passed from mouth to mouth. "It appeared to a shepherd! It was enormous! White!" they will say. They may even exaggerate. They'll have the old man torn to pieces by the wolf's teeth when they tell the legend. The facts will become distorted. The ending will change. The beginning, as well. There'll be hundreds of versions. New characters will appear. But the title will always be the same: the werewolf of the *limits*. In Luiçiana, there's a similar legend. *Wolfman*. A man who becomes a wolf on nights when there's a full moon. It's a curse he carries in his blood. The Romans came to Luiçiana forest with a small contingent. They set up camp. But the forest had been inhabited by a creature since the beginning of time. Gonçaluo Lopes de Luiçiana, sitting on a stone bench in front of his tiny house, tells the story in a hoarse voice with exquisite detail. "*Kracatoa* had the shape of a man, without hair on its body. Its skin was black, the texture like that of a snake. Long fingers. Pointed nails. Sharp teeth. Very quick through the trees. Agile in the dark. The night was its natural habitat. When there's a full moon, it goes out hunting mercilessly." And *Kracatoa* went out to hunt. All the Romans fought against a shadow that devoured them one by one. Their swords were useless. Their spears, as well. They all resisted. And they all died ferociously. All except one, who stood there, waiting for the creature's final attack. He was holding a torch. A flame. *Kracatoa* pounced, but the element of fire frightened it. The soldier waved the torch from side to side. *Kracatoa* retreated, baring its teeth like needles. The soldier had an idea. He would play his last card by sending an arrow of fire to liquidate the beast. And there they were. Squaring up. *Kracatoa* raced towards him. The soldier aimed and fired. The arrow stuck in the body of *Kracatoa*, which started burning all over and shouting in a language that wasn't human. But it doesn't end there. "The soldier went over to the creature's body. He shouldn't have done this. He should have taken to his heels. But he was still impelled by instinct. When he knelt down next to the monster, it was in its death throes. And suddenly, before its last breath, *Kracatoa* pounced and bit the arm of the soldier, who felt a poison passing from the beast's teeth into his bloodstream." That's the curse. Because the soldier survived, but was infected by an illness he felt in his body with fever and sweating. As if something lived on inside him. In his entrails. His ribs. His organs. A monster that will be unleashed on nights when the moon is full. Legends...

The earth of the trail was soft. I could feel it beneath my bare feet. The old man wanted to give me his boots. I refused. I needed to feel the earth on my skin. To let it filter through. Besides, I imagine that was his only footwear. People around here don't possess much. A patched shirt. Trousers held up with a piece of string. Most of them go barefoot. Their feet are black. Their nails, rotten. Children inherit their parents' clothing.

The sky was crazy, because it had stopped raining now, even though it constantly threatened to pour again. The shortcut the old man had shown me entered the wood and then emerged in the meadows. It was a path that climbed cleanly and clearly and came to an end behind the *castro* of Bieiriz.

There were birds in the wood. Melody. The leaves of wet oaks. The odd puddle on the ground, which reflected the landscape like a mirror. A squirrel on a branch, gnawing an acorn with suspicious eyes.

In the meadows, the wind combed the grass, which resisted the movement. I recalled my grandmother's hair. Her long, grey mane. A waterfall. And how she used to comb it from top to bottom. Again and again. Again and again. Again and again. Then she would put it up in a bun. All with excessive care and in exquisite fashion. And all, as well, to conceal that great beauty beneath a black cloth. Beneath the sadness of mourning.

From below, I could see the walls of Bieiriz. The end of the road had turned into a steep path with loose stones. The old man had warned me. "Once you leave the shortcut to one side, you'll have to take the stony road to the *castro*. It's not very long, but it's full of stones." And so it was. My feet were bloody. I missed my shoes. I even missed the boots the old man had offered me. Sometimes my feet were buried beneath stones. Getting them out required a lot of effort. I was sweating. It had started raining again. Heavily.

From that altitude, I could see the thickness of the Valley. The green meadows that surrounded the *castros*. The oak-wood that concealed the nobility of Clear Waters. The cross on Naked Mountain which symbolized Catholic resistance against the Moors' conquest. The ruins of the lookout tower on Horn Peak, a rocky peak that rises in the west. And the small chapel of Our Lady of the Mist, where every year there's a pilgrimage attended by people from distant towns and villages seeking the Virgin's favour.

There was a hole in the wall. A space I could wriggle through. I only just fitted. I scratched a knee on the stone. An elbow, as well.

Bieiriz was made up of circular buildings. Stone walls, nothing else. There was the odd square one. I have to admit it was bigger than it seemed. A well-constructed village. With paths between the buildings like streets. There must have been quite a bit of movement back in the day. Now there's just a silence that sends a shiver down your spine and makes your hair stand on end.

I approached the building emitting smoke. It was the only one with a roof, a thatched roof that seemed to have been repaired recently. That surprised me. The smoke went up. Weakly now. Behind me, a goat. It stared at me. Then leapt over a wall.

I grew tense.

Zzzzzzzzzzzzzzzzzzzzzzzzzzzzzzzz!!        The buzzing of a fly by my ear. In the end, it lands on my arm. I try to crush it, but don't succeed.

Something doesn't feel right.

From the entrance, the inside looks black. A doorway to darkness. I take a silent step. Endeavour to take another. There's not much light inside. The building is almost empty. Without objects. Tables. Chairs. There's a weak, orangish fire on a kind of hearth. That's where the smoke was coming from. A knife on the ground. Two eggs in a rotten basket. And a bag made of animal skin.

Behind      me,      that      growl      again. Grrrrrrrrrrrrrrrrrrrrrrrrrrrrrrrrrrrrrrrrrrrrrrrrrrr...

I didn't want to turn around. I knew what I was going to find. The wolf. It was there. Just like the first time I saw it. Just like the last time. Big. Strong. But, above all, white. The effect of the water on its skin gave it a majestic air. A marble figure. Behind, the silhouette of someone approaching.

## THERE IS A WORD WHICH BEARS
## A SWORD

He was carrying a pile of firewood. I suppose it was to replenish the dying fire. Hanging over his back, he had a rabbit. It was grey. Dead. The wolf was baring its teeth. Always. Rage. The wish to jump on my body and tear me to pieces. I grabbed my knife. The boy let out a whispered "shhhhhhhhhhhhhhhhhhhhhhhhhh". The wolf licked its snout and retreated until it was standing next to its *master*.

The boy fixed me with his gaze. At length. Penetratingly. Breathed calmly and easily. As if he controlled the situation. The wolf. Me...

He entered the building, which may have been a thousand years old. Approached the hearth. Placed the wood next to the fire. Carefully removed the body of the rabbit from his shoulder. Deposited it on the ground.

"How did you find this place?" he asked.

"I suppose I got lucky," I replied ironically.

He smiled faintly. Combed his hair to one side with his fingertips. It covered one eye. He repeated the gesture a couple of times.

"I don't think so," he leant against a wall. "What are you going to do now? Hand me over to the authorities?"

"You saved me from the Alvariz twins and the Collector…"

He raised his eyebrows.

"Saved you?" he continued. "I didn't save you from anything. I killed them because I had to. That's how it had to be. They were next on the list."

The wolf approached. Brushed against the boy's waist. The boy stroked it. Softly. Delicately. And the animal lay on the ground, seeking the fire's weak warmth. The boy grabbed some branches of firewood and started placing them on the fire. Then he passed a finger over the wolf's snout. From top to bottom. The wolf seemed to like it.

"Headbreaker told me your father turned up dead. He had problems with the Count on account of land. Did they murder him?"

Grrrrrrrrrrrrrrrrrrrrrrr, the wolf. Shhhhhhhhhhhhhhhhhhhhhhhh, him.

"No. It was me. Or rather him," he pointed at the wolf. "But he and I are one and the same. A prolongation."

I couldn't understand. Opposite me was a boy who replied sometimes as if I wasn't there. As if it was a voice coming out of some corner of the building.

"Why? He was your father... wasn't he?"

He took one of the branches and poked the burning logs. I stared at the fire and couldn't help having a vision. Once again. Images that appear between flashes of light. The *jungle*. That night. And the fire going out on skin. I observed their shouts of pain as they writhed about.

"Old de Souza, as he's known in the Valley, was a son of a bitch," he replied. "He raped my mother, who was a native. He never tired of saying this. And months after she gave birth, he grabbed me like some kind of object and brought me over to this side of the world. He was the first to die."

I was confused. I wanted to direct thousands of questions towards this permanently unenthusiastic boy, who had surprised me the first time I'd seen him in Headbreaker's tavern, serving wine with a defiant expression. But I didn't know where to begin. I didn't know whether the wolf would get up and leap on top of me. Sink its teeth in. Drag me from side to side... Pain. I can't avoid the pain. The pain is always there. I'm afraid of it.

"And Mateu Pelaiz, did you kill him as well?"

"Yes."

He didn't hesitate. The image he projected in the *castro* had nothing to do with the wine server from Headbreaker's. Here, he seemed like a grown-up, fully built. He even commanded respect. His voice was firm and confident. Rigid.

"He was a blind man who could barely stand up. Was it necessary?"

"Yes. It was necessary. He was the Count's previous collector. Very loyal to the House of Guimaraes. A fanatic of the *King*. Then, the *Queen*. He was cruel. Violent. Men have their past, Mr d'Ourantes. The fact they're old doesn't justify a pardon for everything they've done."

"So what are you? Some kind of justice seeker?"

He smiled. I could see his teeth this time. The wolf stood up. Walked around me. I followed its footsteps in a state of tension. It went back to its *master*.

"No. I'm not a justice seeker. This is revenge. Something that makes me feel good. Me against them. It's got nothing to do with justice. It's the satisfaction of killing those you believe have done you harm. Revenge. You know about that, don't you? You burnt them all."

His last words beat against me. Penetrated my brain like needles passing through flesh and bone. Fire. Screams. And suddenly I felt my body was cold. My vision was blurred. My legs buckled. I was weak. I could barely stay on my feet. I knelt down on the ground. The boy didn't flinch. Nor did the wolf. I found it difficult to swallow air. I saw everything falling on top of me. "Calm down. Breathe. Calm down. Take it easy," I kept saying to myself. And the world, which was whizzing past, began to return to its place.

"I ha... ha... have to get out... Ha... have to get out of here. Es... escape. The bishop... the bishop will be... looking for me..."

Every time I spoke, I felt a stabbing in my heart.

"Don't worry about Bishop del Riego. He's dead. He received our visit around midnight. And I can assure you, from the scene I encountered when I opened the door of his room, he won't be stepping in the land of his *God*."

In certain circles of the Valley, it was rumoured that the bishop liked very young women. Girls. The Alvariz twins went looking for them in villages. Paid off their parents. Took them to the bishop's room in red cloaks. Their faces covered in masks that imitated stags' heads. Gave them crowns made of the stags' own antlers. And at midnight left them carefully on the silk sheets of the bishop's bed. Del Riego would appear at another door, almost naked, a wolf's mask hiding his features, a wolf's tail tied to his waist. Repulsive. Vomit-inducing. The boy must have caught the bishop in one of those horrifying scenes. I imagine the wolf ripping the greasy flesh of the bishop, who is dressed as a wolf. Del Riego screaming in pain. And I feel satisfaction. Depraved monster.

The boy picked up the bag and rolled it up. He then tied it with a piece of string and threw it on his back. He did the same with the rabbit. Extinguished the fire. And headed towards the door. The wolf went after him. I followed on my knees, trying to recover and catch my breath. I saw his upright silhouette illuminated by the frail light. The rain started falling again.

"Wait!" I lifted my hand. "How... how... ho... how do you do it? Where... wh... where did you learn... that? To... to... control the wolf."

Outside, through the sound of the rain, could be heard a crow. Cruuuuuuuuaaaaghhh! The wind started rising and stirring everything that succumbed to its movement. The boy looked outside. The scene didn't seem to disturb him. A thin mist floated over the ground, slowly invading the space.

"There are things that can't be explained, Mr d'Ourantes. Things one has in one's insides from the day one is born. Qualities embedded in the blood like an inheritance. I found him lost in the middle of the wood," he looked at the wolf and stroked its back, "and at that same moment a link arose between us. We were children. Both in our own way. Me, a boy. Him, a wolf. But both of us animals. And then everything happens in here," he placed a palm on his chest. "In here. Inside. Inside me. Inside him. We are one and the same," he glanced at the wolf.

From my perspective, the figure of the boy and the wolf were in shadow because of the contrast in light between the inside and outside of the building. Two shadows with impenetrable, even heroic traits, but also terrifying and mysterious. The boy turned around and mounted the wolf like it was a horse. That amazed me. I'd never seen that before. And suddenly a storm exploded to add even more mystery to the scene.

"Your name... Your name is Tarthai?"

He placed a hand on the wolf's back. His fingers sank into the white fur. He twisted around towards me. The wind lifted his hair, which covered his face at times. He didn't push it aside, he just let it be. The silhouettes of the boy and the wolf – or as he'd said, two animals – were lit by a flash of lightning.

"Yes," he replied. "Just like your son..."

And he surged into the rain on the wolf's back. I lay there on the ground, taking in his answer. Even though inside the building the water wasn't getting in anywhere, inside my body a deep sorrow began to spill over. Tarthai.

# THE UNIVERSE IS STILL

Slaughter is on the other side of the Valley. It's a small town located on stony, infertile land. The inhabitants are not allowed to work or hunt on the Count's properties. To use the royal thoroughfares. Or to take water from their fountains. And so on until the fourth generation of rebels. Headbreaker calls them "trash". "In Slaughter, there's only trash, stones, and sand," and then he lets out a laugh that reverberates through the tavern.

They only just get by. Day after day. This means they will feed on anything. Rats. Cats. Dogs. There's even a rumour that says the dead aren't buried in Slaughter, they're tossed on the barbecue. Stories. The town isn't as wretched as it appears. They have allies who help them. Organizations that don't agree with the system and wait in the shadows to make the transition to power and change everything.

This was the place the men who supported and survived the *Revolt of the Sickles* were expelled to. They arrived and built a town with their own bare hands in an area that was hostile by nature. Children, grandchildren, great-grandchildren, and great-great-grandchildren paid – and will pay – for their ancestors' mistakes. It's a sentence that seems eternal. Even so, hatred is also inherited. Stories are handed down. Ideology, as well. They detest the monarchy. The nobility and landowners. But, above all, they detest the Church. Most of the inhabitants are pagans, even though they don't admit this because they know they'll end up hanging at the Gates of Holy Victory.

An old woman is sitting on a stump next to the door of her house. She gives me a defiant look. Doesn't say a word. I imitate her. They're distrustful. The people. Here. They wonder, "What's he doing in Slaughter? Is he a spy of the Count's or the *Queen's*?"

I opened the door to *Sickles* inn. It's not really called that. That's a secret name. A form of code. People being pursued by the authorities tend to hide there. People who, like the inhabitants of Slaughter, repudiate the system. It's the meeting place for the *peasant army*, a movement that carries out small acts of rebellion against the landowners in favour of the peasants' right to land. The last thing they did was burn two cornfields belonging to the Marquis of Mudlands. The fact is these acts always have negative consequences for the peasants, because the landowners take it out on them and demand they make up for their losses.

Inside the inn is a man behind the bar with an excessively serious expression. There's also a dog resting on the floor. It appears to be very old. Patches of hair are missing all over its body. Its ears are chewed by flies. It has wounds. It gets up slowly. Ambles over to the far side of the inn.

"Good morning."

The man didn't say anything. He turned and started cleaning the furniture behind him.

"A day ago," I continued, "a girl called Briana should have arrived here."

"I don't know anything about it," he replied.

"I'm not an enemy of Slaughter. It was me who told her to come here. In fact, I'm the one who helped her escape."

There was a silence. Then the man turned around. He was heavy and had this plait that went down to his waist. A badly trimmed beard. He was wearing a white shirt that was covered in shit. He grabbed a knife and brandished it in his fist.

"I don't know what you're talking about. I told you already!" he fixed me with a stare. "What's your name?"

"Lourenço d'Ourantes."

"The wolf hunter?"

"Among other things, it could be said..."

"Who did you say you were asking after?"

I felt he was taking the mickey. I remained calm.

"A girl called Briana. More or less this high," I indicated her height with the palm of my hand. "Dressed in an overcoat. And a yellowish, bloodstained nightdress. Pale skin. She's thirteen."

The man propped an elbow on the counter. Stroked the beard that gathered under his chin. Became thoughtful. Twisted his lips to one side. Gazed at the ceiling.

"No! There's been nobody here of that description," he raised his arms. "I'm very sorry. I can't help you," and he went back to doing what he'd been doing before I came in through that accursed door.

He was lying. That much was clear. He was lying. You could see it by his gestures. The words that hummed in his mouth. His look that opposed mine. Small details. Tiny, almost imperceptible details. He was lying.

The inn was almost empty. There were only four wooden tables with their respective stools. And, to drink, they served this poor-quality, homemade pulque. There was no wine. Or beer. I thought about Víctor, the *stranger*, and what a tough time he'd have had if we'd met here instead of the House of the Viços.

"Listen," I continued, "you have to believe me. I know Briana…"

"Three Wolves?" an aged voice came from the far end of the tavern. "Is that you?"

An old man was sitting in the corner. With his back to me. All I could see was a bald patch and long, white hair falling down the sides. He didn't turn around. I went over to him. The floorboards creaked beneath my boots. One step. Two steps. An elderly gentleman sitting on a stool. He was blind. Finding it hard to breathe. He wore a chestnut-brown tunic that had been repaired numerous times. His wrinkled hands held onto a boxwood stick. His skin was covered in spots and scars. He should have been dead, but seemed reluctant to leave this world.

"Who are you?"

The old man smiled. And then adopted a look of amazement.

"I'd recognize that voice anywhere. But it cannot be. You're... you should be dead already. It... it's... impossible. My *God*!" he made the sign of the cross. "My *God*!"

I grabbed a stool and sat beside him. Moved closer to his face. Trying to make out every detail. Discover who it was. The old man raised a hand and passed it over my face in an attempt to discern my features by means of his fingertips. He moved it slowly. A ray of light passed through the window and made this gesture almost paternal.

"Yes, yes, it's you. Three Wolves. This... this must be the work of..."

I put a hand on his mouth as if to stop the word that was about to come out. Shhhhhhhhhhhhhhhhhhh!! The old man nodded and leant backwards.

"Who are you?" I repeated softly.

The old man put his arms on the table. And slowly pulled back the cloth that covered his left arm. He was missing a hand. His arm only reached as far as his wrist.

"Martiño de Braga!" I cried. "My *God*! I thought you were dead, old friend! How old are you?"

"Ninety-three last autumn. You're the one who should be below ground," he let out a guffaw and then coughed deeply. "It's unbelievable!"

Martiño de Braga was the other wolf hunter at the time of the business in White Cliffs. We'd both been hired by the brothers of White Cliffs Monastery to hunt the wolf. To start with, we had lots of disagreements. He used ancient, homemade methods. I used the *link* from the *jungle*. But when the first boy turned up dead in a maize field, we got down to work. People were getting frightened. There were stories of demons coming out at night to take away the souls of children. Martiño had a tattoo of a wolf whose head occupied the back of his hand. The wolf tore it off the night we discovered the massacre.

"Tell me, old friend... What are you doing in this accursed land of Slaughter?"

I brought my lips close to the old man's ear. The barman didn't take his eyes off us. He was on the alert.

"A girl. Briana. I helped her escape the dungeons of Constança palace. Told her to come here so she would be safe. But that guy over there," I gestured towards the bar with my thumb, "says there's been nobody of that name here. And of course I don't believe him."

Martiño raised his eyebrows. Leant on his stick and stood up. I got up quickly to help him, but he refused. "No, I can manage on my own!" He dragged his feet. They were bare. The barman watched him approaching.

"It's him. Bring the girl."

"But you said that was impossible..."

"It's him!" he shouted loudly. "Bring the girl!"

"Yes, Sparrow. Whatever you say."

The barman went out of a back door. Old Martiño stood there with his knees bent. He was the sparrow.

The leader of the *peasant army*. The one who set its objectives. He looked too old to me for such a position of responsibility. He was blind. Missing a hand. But there's a lot of respect for hierarchy in these parts. Wisdom. And until Martiño de Braga went to a better place, he would be the sparrow.

"So you're the *peasant army's* sparrow," I said.

He nodded.

"Yes, old friend. Who would have thought it? Me, a defender of the old *King*. Remember?"

"I remember. What was it that changed everything?"

Martiño pointed to a stool so I would give it to him and he could sit down. I brought it over and helped him to lower himself. He took a deep breath. And then coughed. Heavily. Leant on my arm. And stared at me with the eyes of a blind centenarian.

"Something always happens in the life of a man for everything to be turned around. A moment. An event. We leave behind what we believe in order to believe the opposite. And become more radical. Harder. Ready to die for our ideals. You know what took place in the Limit with the epidemic?"

I nodded. The story was well known. It reached every vertex of the *Kingdom*. Tragic stories are difficult to forget, despite the years. They stay there, in a damp corner. Stored away. Like an object at the back of a drawer. Nobody knows how it began. They say it was a larva that got in the potatoes and laid its eggs there. Others talk about the river water. Whatever it was, the effects of the *epidemic* on the human body were disastrous. It started with a light fever. Then vomiting. Bleeding from the mouth. Rotting. The body couldn't take its food. It gradually withered away. Very slowly. Very slowly. Very slowly. Until it was just skin and bones. They left the villages in order to move to other lands in search of help. Doctors. Medicine. Nobody wanted them in case they passed on the illness. And so they stayed there. In limbo. Dying.

"I see them with these eyes that are now blind," he continued. "I'd been hired from the County of Baleah to hunt a wolf. A few sheep had turned up dead. Nothing out of this world. To get to Baleah, there's no better route than crossing the Limit from east to west," Martiño sighed, it was as if he wished to recall the images despite the years, and I'm sure he remembered them so exactly, so clearly, that they sent a shiver down his spine. "I saw them from the summit. High up. Thousands of people gathered together, old friend. Boys. Girls. Fathers. Mothers. Grandfathers. Grandmothers. Families. Skeletons. Hardly any skin. They walked as if they had no soul. They'd set up a kind of camp. They slept in the open. Cold. With nothing. That... whatever it was, had turned them into corpses. That's what they were, yellow corpses. And nobody did a thing. Nobody, anywhere, not here, or in the adjoining Counties, or in the capital. Not a thing! They all left them to die. All of them. In order then to set fire to the bodies lying in heaps, rotting on the ground. Some embracing their loved ones. A mother, a child. A newly-wed couple. Others on their own, solitary, leaning against the trunk of some tree, patiently awaiting their end while staring at the sky with open mouth," he was silent for a moment, immersed in his own thoughts.

"What kind of world is this, eh? Tell me, Lourenço!" he banged the table. "What kind of *King* lets his people die in such cruel fashion? No. That's not the way. We have to destroy the system. Blow it up. Use dynamite. Whatever the cost."

Martiño gazed at the floor. A cockroach passed next to his feet. He let it be. That insect had nothing to do with it. It wasn't to blame for what was happening in this repulsive world. I could understand the old man. Understand his reasoning. He was right. That's true. But I'm no one to talk. I did terrible things. Acts that will lead me directly to hell.

Someone came crashing into the inn.

"The bishop! The bishop! He's dead! Del Riego is dead!" he shouted.

And suddenly that room filled with people dancing about with joy. Singing. Smiling.

"He turned up dead, Sparrow!" they shouted into Martiño's ear. "In his bed. His innards spilling out. Everything in the open!"

The old man grinned. Several of them lifted him up and carried him into the middle of the crowd. Martiño rose above the heads of the assembled company. Gestured to be let down. People started bandying about sentences like "it's time to attack", "we'll win", "we'll put an end to this tyranny". Words of hope that, in the twinkling of an eye, end up underground, while the same people as always come out on top. Again. And again. And again. And so on until the end.

# TRUE POEMS FLEE

Briana was a different person. Another girl. In a couple of days, a spectacular metamorphosis had taken place. She no longer looked innocent and timid. Afraid. Not anymore. I suppose in that time she'd crossed the line. That thin, almost imperceptible strip that marks the transition from being a girl to being a woman. There, in those eyebrows, eyes, red hue of the cheeks, thick lips... there wasn't a girl. Oh, no. There was a woman. Shapely. Strong. Determined. Ready to start a fire. To do away with everything.

"You're sure you don't want to come? I don't mind taking you. Honestly."

She traced a shy smile that couldn't hide the wounds she'd suffered up until that moment. It's something that will remain there always. In her. It won't heal. Being obliged to leave her home, her parents. To work in the Count's palace. To go hungry. Cold. Hostile treatment. The twins' rape. Imprisonment. Abuse. Threats. The Collector's knife on her neck. Tears. Solitary flight to Slaughter. Fear. No. That wound won't close. It'll bleed forever. And bleed. And bleed. Over and over, again and again… until her veins are empty of blood. There's nothing left. Nothing at all.

"It's my duty, Mr d'Ourantes."

"This is a dangerous place. And you… You're still… you're still only a girl! Don't think…"

Briana didn't let me finish the sentence. She threw herself on me in a tight hug. Pressed her head against my chest. I embraced her narrow waist in my arms. Stroked her hair. And in the bottom of my stomach arose again a paternal feeling that hadn't been awake in ages. A long time. The *jungle*. Tarthai.

"I have to stay here," she looked at me with moist eyes, repressing her emotion. "There are lots of girls on their own, like me. Outside. Women in this world of men, exposed to their desires. It's not fair. I have to try and save them. Rescue them from this imposed sentence. I don't want them to go through what I went through. I don't want them to suffer. I have to act. It's the best decision."

Briana had joined the *peasant army*. She had it in her head. The ideas and so on. The ideology. Deep inside her brain. She will devote her life to what she believes is right. She doesn't realize justice is double-edged. Here, they fill your head with idyllic worlds. Perfect, objective worlds. A cause and a purpose. But that is followed by reality. And reality is where you have to fight. Because the biggest problem about human beings is human beings themselves. Us.

One of the boys in the inn was watching her. He didn't realize I'd noticed his spontaneous gestures. Perhaps he was in love with her. He was a little older than Briana. He looked like a good enough kid. Though you never know. I imagined he was the one who'd persuaded her to stay. Who'd talked to her of a better society without people going hungry. Without *Kings*. Or nobles. Or landowners. A place of peace. Young people are like that. They want to change the world from one day to the next. But everything has its time.

"Where are you going now?" asked Briana.

"Me? To Luiçiana! That's my home."

"I wouldn't recommend it..." said a third voice behind.

I turned around. In front of me was a man wearing a kind of beret with a small red circle embroidered on the front. The symbol of the *peasant army*. He held out his arm to shake my hand. I did the same.

"Ares d'Almeida, sir," he introduced himself. "I'm one of the *army's* four generals."

I stared at him incredulously. He had a rifle slung over his shoulder. He might have been a peasant who'd got involved when he was young. In the movement. And little by little acquired power. He didn't look much like a general.

"Why wouldn't you recommend that I go back to Luiçiana?"

He removed the rifle from his shoulder and leant on it.

"The *Queen* sent troops to take control of it. She wants it to form part of a new bishopric in the interior. The inhabitants of Luiçiana are resisting, hiding in the thickness of the wood. They attack at night. But the troops have already taken a lot of land. What can they do against armed soldiers? They're killing them. Gunning them down. They cover their eyes. Tie their hands. And shoot. Then leave the bodies in the open. Stop the families going to collect them to give them a proper funeral. Leave them to rot on the grass. It's terrible."

I closed my eyes and imagined all those people fighting. Dying, as well. I couldn't help recalling the odd battle I'd taken part in. I was on the other side. The side of the troops. A soldier. We were merciless. I might have been the worst of them all. I took pleasure in pain. Suffering. Fed on that. Took pleasure in war. Feeling invincible. *God*.

"I don't care. I'm going back to Luiçiana."

# 'TIS LIVING HURTS US MORE

Auuuuuuuuuuuuuuuuuuuuuuuuuuuuuuuuu! The wolf can be heard on this night of open shirts. The stars are white signs on a cloak of mourning like the one Grandma used to wear. She. Alone. Always alone. And quiet. Not saying anything. Carrying the burden. The suffering. At night, she would shelter me in the warmth of her arms. Sing me a song to send me to sleep. Then cry. I realized. She wept for all the ones she'd lost. Wept because of their absence. Now I understand it all.

A shooting star divides the night. Appears and disappears in the twinkling of an eye. Impossible to make a wish. Just one. Nothing more.

The fire was going out. Fire. Always fire. In the pupils. As they shouted. Revenge. It's inevitable.

I tossed a couple of branches into the flames. The horse was on its feet. Still. Merging with the darkness. It looked like a painting. The wood played a nocturnal melody. The sounds are easy to distinguish. Wind. Oak branches colliding. Little owls. Insects. Then there are those that are indecipherable. Better not to know what they are. In the wood, there are creatures. Strange, dangerous creatures. In the *jungle*, we were the strange ones. The dangerous ones, as well.

I could see memory in the fire. In the red and orange hues. I could see my whole life. Eternal. A childhood spent running through the trees. My father's shouts on arriving home. Mother washing the clothes in the river. Grandma, sad. I could see the battles. The blades I'd stuck in the bodies of other men. A life snatched. Blood. The atrocities I'd committed. I could see the *jungle*. The rays sliding through the forest. Children prancing about naked. Rain. The snake moving slowly. The mixture of sounds. Lizah. Tarthai. Zoriah. Fire.

Tras!

Somebody stepped on a branch on the ground. I turned around. There she was again. The *Eadar* in the same white dress. With the same crown of flowers. She seemed illuminated by a light that wasn't of this world. An angelic image.

She sat down beside me. Delicately. Crossed her legs, which were illuminated by the beautiful light of the fire.

"So, you're going back to Luiçiana?" she said.

I took a stick. Poked the logs with it, keeping my eyes on the fire.

"I am. It's my place."

She looked at me.

"Your place is not this. You're not here, remember. You're in the *jungle*."

She touched me on the chest. And again I felt that force inside. Like in Valley Arch, after coming down from Snowy Peak. She got inside me. And saw everything once more. I couldn't help crying because of the emergence of hidden memories and feelings. A spiral ascending from the depths and destroying everything in its path. I felt like throwing up. Spitting it all out.

"Why do you do this to me? I don't want... I don't want to remember. No, I don't. Too much pain," I said as the tears coursed down my cheeks. "Too many memories."

"Pain is part of us. We cause it. Suffer it. A human quality. We have to learn to live with it. To assimilate it."

"I can't bear it. I can't bear it anymore. The pain. It consumes me. It devours me from within. After all this time, it's still there, day after day. And I'm still here, day after day, as well. You know how many times I've tried to put an end to all this? Do you?" I opened my shirt and showed her all the scars. All the marks on my body. The signs of wanting to put an end to all this. Life. But I can't.

The *Eadar* stroked the scars. Slowly. Traced them with her finger like they were a map. A map of the attempts to leave everything behind. To surrender to the pain. A map of a death that never was. Never will be.

"How can I finish this?" I begged in desperation. "How can I finish all this? Do you know? How can I...

When will it end...?" I started sobbing on the *Eadar's* legs, like a child seeking its mother's consolation.

She combed my hair, as if wanting to give it meaning. But nothing has meaning. Nothing.

"Until you feel the same sorrow, until you feel the same pain..." she answered.

Read more fiction in English from Small Stations Press:

## Abel TOMÉ, NIGHT OF THE CROW

The island of Gothard is a law unto itself. Separated from the mainland by a long bridge, it has its own chancellor and popular jury. The island is run by two powerful families, the Faols (who own the silver mine) and the Cárthaigs (who own the bank). Decisions are taken by popular vote in the main square, Wolf Tongue. But when the schoolteacher and his family turn up dead in the house next to the lighthouse, Beth police force is called to the scene. The inspector in charge of the case is Gonçalves. He lives in Beth, a city that has two faces according to how much money you have, though he originally hails from Galataz in the north of the country. He is haunted by the memory of his wife, Anne Marie. The other officers on the case are Pietre, a sex addict who smokes too much, and Lúa, whose father suffers from Alzheimer's and whose great-grandfather was from the island. Aidan Faol, the chancellor, doesn't take kindly to outside interference, and Gonçalves will need to have all his wits about him if he is to get to the truth of why the schoolteacher and his family were murdered. This will involve unearthing some dirty secrets about the island itself and will force Gonçalves to confront his own past in one of the best crime novels to have come out of Galicia in the last twenty years.

ISBN 978-954-384-137-0

## Diego AMEIXEIRAS, NIGHT OF THE CAIMAN

In *Night of the Caiman*, a writer, Ricardo Barros, seeks to complete his magnum opus and in the process to recreate something of the life of David Goodis. He will even move to Goodis' native Philadelphia to follow in his footsteps and discover something of the darker corners that this city contains. His teacher in the art of writing is Vicente Mallón, pseudonym Vincent Malone, whose secretary, Selma, the daughter of a local policeman, will also end up in Philly, seeking the lost treasure that she lovingly handed over to a man who was not deserving of her trust. Each paragraph in this narrative has been painstakingly constructed. The book in its entirety serves as a tribute to all the authors and filmmakers – from David Goodis to Dashiell Hammett and Patricia Highsmith, François Truffaut and Paul Wendkos – who with their work and devotion to their craft have gifted us hours of entertainment.

ISBN 978-954-384-139-4

## Rosa ANEIROS, RESISTANCE

Rosa Aneiros' novel *Resistance* is an epic of contemporary Galician literature that follows the fortunes of two very different people during the Estado Novo, the authoritarian regime in Portugal under António Salazar and Marcello Caetano that lasted from 1933 to 1974. Dinis Cardoso is a glass-factory worker from a small fishing village on Portugal's west coast, São Pedro de Moel. He will be conscripted for the Colonial War in Mozambique. An attempt to stand up for workers' rights will land him in the infamous Peniche political prison. Filipa Rodrigues is a privileged girl growing up in Coimbra. Her father, Rui Rodrigues, is a successful importer of goods who has made his own fortune. He leans politically towards the right, but his daughter's activities in the resistance will force the family to flee to Brazil. Sometimes events take precedence over our own wishes – our paths diverge, seemingly never to meet again – and memories are like the breakers on São Pedro de Moel beach, pulled under and out to sea. The novel examines political events in Portugal during the twentieth century, and the influence these events had on ordinary people, in a way that is strikingly reminiscent of Gabriel García Márquez's *One Hundred Years of Solitude*.

ISBN 978-954-384-138-7

For an up-to-date list of our publications, please visit www.smallstations.com

Printed by BoD™in Norderstedt, Germany